THE EXPLOITS OF BEAU QUICKSILVER

The Apes of Devil's Island

BY JOHN CUNNINGHAM

The Darkness at Windon Manor

BY MAX BRAND

The Flying Legion

BY GEORGE ALLAN ENGLAND

The Golden Cat:
The Adventures of Peter the Brazen, Volume 3

BY LORING BRENT

The Opposing Venus: The Complete Cabalistic Cases
of Semi Dual, the Occult Detector

BY J.U. GIESY AND JUNIUS B. SMITH

The Radio Menace

BY RALPH MILNE FARLEY

The Ruby of Suratan Singh: The Adventures
of Scarlet and Bradshaw, Volume 2

BY THEODORE ROSCOE

The Sheriff of Tonto Town:
The Complete Tales of Sheriff Henry, Volume 2

BY W.C. TUTTLE

The Vengeance of the Wah Fu Tong:
The Complete Cases of Jigger Masters, Volume 1

BY ANTHONY M. RUD

THE EXPLOITS OF BEAU QUICKSILVER

FLORENCE M. PETTEE

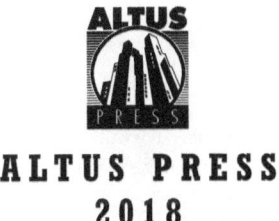

ALTUS PRESS
2018

PUBLISHING HISTORY

"The Exploits of Beau Quicksilver" originally appeared in the February 24, March 3,
   10, 17, 24, 31, and April 7, 1923 issues of *Argosy* magazine (Vol. 149, No. 4–Vol.
   150, No. 4). Copyright © 1923 by The Frank A. Munsey Company. Copyright
   renewed © 1950 and assigned to Steeger Properties, LLC. All rights reserved.

THANKS TO

Joel Frieman and Joseph Laturnau

Visit *altuspress.com* for more books like this.

TABLE OF CONTENTS

A TOOTH FOR A TOOTH

THE BIG BULK of the chief spat a number into the phone receiver. The line simmered under the heat of his intonation.

Came the tantalizing drawl of Central, "They don't answer."

"I tell you," roared the chief, "I know he's there. Hold your thumb on. Throw a light there! Wake up!"

In an aside he rasped to an assistant, "He must be there. Just in from that Everglades murder—"

There was a rattle on the wire.

"What's that?" demanded the irate police head.

"They don't answer," repeated the girl at Central with blithe scorn.

The chief banged up the receiver. "Here, Dean, take my place. Keep on eye peeled for anything doing. I'll go over myself. Damnation! Where is that fellow Quicksilver?"

"That no one but Quicksilver himself knows—*unless he chooses*, you can bet," swung back the chief's understudy.

"I'll find out," rapped that impatient dignitary. "Got to get him instanter. This Whitney case is too big to be bungled—can't let any one take a sniff at it but Quicksilver. Queer business!"

Chief Cartman slammed the door after him. He flung himself into his car waiting at the curb. He stepped on the gas until the motor shot ahead like an enraged comet. It reminded him of Beau Quicksilver on the chase—playing a hunch with every nerve strung to capacity speed and acuteness. For the exquisite detective—"that damned dude dick" to the under-

1

world—was an enigmatical crime chaser—a mercurial mystery master. Like a chimerical will-of-the-wisp, he lunged to the answer in each cryptic case. No wonder they clubbed him Quicksilver. He ran through a fellow's fingers just like mercury. There had never been another sleuth like him—not even a forty-second cousin to him. No one could fathom how he landed the goods. His methods were just that elusive.

And finical! Why, a spoiled operatic star couldn't equal him for temperament! The fellow wouldn't touch a case with the tip of his nobbiest cane if the thing didn't interest him. They couldn't beg, hire or steal him to it.

"Nothing doing!" he would call back with languid insolence, as he irritatingly flipped the ashes from some imported cigarette end. "That crime smells stale at the outset. It's racy Roquefort or nothing!" And when Beau Quicksilver opined thus it meant finis. The case was dead for him. But when some baffling mystery turned up! Ah, then the scintillating sparks flew! There was a flash of Quicksilver. Followed the startling showdown!

The chief left his car at the curb. He pushed viciously at a button in the brown stone apartment. The bell went singing sibilantly through the house.

There was an irritating, arrogant wait. Cartman jabbed an encore at the bell.

Then a slight, gray-clad servant opened the door with ludicrous caution. He spoke in a whisper. Unquestionably Quicksilver's man, Shunta, regarded his elusive, temperamental master with great awe. But his hero worship was catered to only at arm's length by the coolly aloof Quicksilver. Shunta's fearful adulation suggested the deep-down admiration of the small boy for Georges Carpentier, or the gawky-legged girl's first devotion to Maude Adams.

"Where is he?" demanded the chief. "Isn't he here? Why doesn't he—"

"Yes," gently admonished Shunta. "He's here. Only he ordered me to stuff the telephone. And not until your second-ring at the door here would he let me answer. 'That's Cartman,' he said. 'Thinks he's steering a real crime here. Tell by the way his thumb stuttered on the second jab at the bell. Shunta,' he told me, 'inform the chief of police that it's just two minutes to spill the new idea. Not a second longer unless it's real mystery and not some bludgeoning bump-off!'"

Fuming internally, the chief went up behind the pussy-footed Shunta. He didn't relish the coming scene. For Beau Quicksilver was a veritable tiger when in one of his moods. Yet again he would weep at the mere sound of pathetic music. An obtuse riddle, Quicksilver! A regular Sphinx at times, and then affably human. Nobody ever knew where to find him next.

With awed deference Shunta bowed the chief in. Cartman shut the door firmly behind him. The room was darkened by drawn shades.

Then a blinding flash of light seared the darkness.

A cool, domineering, petulant voice ordered, "Go back and shut that door again! Make it soft—pianissimo. *Pronto!* Where do you think you are? In a blacksmith's shop? Well, you can cut out the anvil chorus here."

A figure lay on the luxurious couch. There was a tall glass on the taboret beside him. He was clad in the most elegant of silk pyjamas. Imported Chinese embroidered sandals covered the feet. There was a bandage under the thatch of thick, but carefully brushed hair. Yet the line of linen could not conceal the height of the forehead. The dead white accentuated the smoldering, almost feverish brilliancy of the tired gray eyes. The purple shadows of complete exhaustion lay beneath the fiery orbs. Despite the fatigued and fretful lines on the oval face, the features stood forth delicate, sensitive, but baffling in their elusive suggestion of hidden strength. And the jaw whispered of the martial force of a Napoleon.

"What do you want?" querulously inquired Beau Quicksilver, with weak, lackluster interest. "Can't you see I'm done to a frazzle? If you have come here on some fool's chase, I'll throw you out of the window."

This suggestion from a mere bag of fluff, tipping the scales at one hundred and fifty-five pounds, caused the big chief an acute attack of internal merriment. His quick anger receded before the amusing, bantamweight idea.

Then unbidden Cartman helped himself to one of the Sheraton chairs in the fastidiously furnished apartment.

But Beau Quicksilver wasn't even regarding him. The detective smoked as though it were a physical effort even to expel the thin circles of consuming tobacco.

The chief leaned forward purposively. He breathed of leonine strength. He spoke with the staccato incisiveness of a rapid-fire gun.

"Just got a hurry call to the Whitney house."

Beau Quicksilver stopped smoking. The cigarette dangled forgotten from his fingers. At last the sleuth's burning eyes were on the big man from headquarters.

"It's murder!" rapped Cartman.

The fastidious figure sat up. He tossed the cigarette onto a copper tray.

"Cyrus Whitney has been done for—shot to death in his den," finished the chief.

Beau Quicksilver leaped from the couch. He ripped off the bandage. He sped like some unleashed thing gripped in the fury of an overwhelming urge.

Fatigue had dropped from him like a cloak. The peevish irritability of a moment before had vanished. It was as though dark and rumbling clouds had suddenly been blown away by a whiff of quickening ozone. Again the air was surcharged with mystery. It quickened him like some dose of super-strychnine.

The new and rejuvenated Beau Quicksilver plunged through a door, kicking off his slippers into the room. He moved like a dart from a joyously strung bow.

"I'll be with you in a jiffy, Cartman," he called out blithely. "Just let me fall into this new tweed suit of mine."

Fifteen minutes later a completely rehabilitated Quicksilver left the house for the Whitney mansion and the major crime it concealed.

CHAPTER II

SOME UNIFORMED MEN saluted respectfully as Quicksilver slid past them to the main door of the Whitney house. The place was one of the show spots. The big banker, now cold in violent death, had been a financial power of the first magnitude.

"Rotten business, sir," greeted a man from headquarters.

He guarded the death chamber, a room at the rear of the house on the first floor. It was known as the dead banker's favorite study. It had appealed to him because of its quiet location. Thick trees dotted the fine lawns outside. And there was a high wall surrounding the estate. Cyrus Whitney had loved night solitude as a tonic from the wear and tear of momentous daily affairs.

Beau Quicksilver nodded abstractedly to the would-be agreeable comment of the blue-clad figure. "Don't let me be disturbed by any one, Daniels. You understand. I want to be alone with my thoughts—*where it happened.*"

"I get you," was the reply. "I'll fend them off. Trust me."

"Thanks, Daniels. I do."

Without another word the lithe, tan-clad figure of Beau Quicksilver entered the silent room. The hush of death was upon it. The air breathed of the untoward. It smelled of crime.

Quicksilver stood just inside the door. His thin nostrils were dilated. His deep eyes seemed unconscious of the magnificent furnishings—and of that stark, cold figure, once dominant in high finance, but now laid low by the Czar of Violent Death. For a moment he stood motionless. Then he shrugged his slim shoulders. Slowly his gaze swept the room.

He saw the heavy drawn shades. He noted the massive book-cases lining two of the walls almost to the ceiling. Evidently the dead man had been a lover of literature as well as a money master. He saw the heavily upholstered furniture depressing the thick pile of the carpet. Then his eyes went to the figure of the dead man.

Cyrus Whitney's body sagged forward on a huge mahogany desk near the middle of the room. His velvet dressing jacket, gray in tone, bore an ugly brown splotch which spread out in the vicinity of the heart. The utter abandon of the pose suggested that he had died instantly—had fallen forward a dead weight. The chair was rather close to the desk. Dishes were scattered about at rakish angles upon it. A damask napkin, grimly splashed with brown, dangled disconsolately from one of the stiff knees.

Beau Quicksilver strode forward a step. This was not common death—the finding of a body amid the broken dishes and the nearly devoured viands of a hearty meal. Rigorously ignoring further details on the littered desk top, he examined the body itself.

Cyrus Whitney had been shot through the heart—a clean-cut, expert shot with a medium caliber revolver, seeming a .32. Death must have been instantaneous.

Slowly the detective's eyes went to the objects on the desk. The mahogany had evidently been freed of papers and workaday things for the coming of the late repast. A small platter showed a mere fragment of chicken; there were scraps of potatoes and vegetables. The salad plate was empty. The coffee cup lay smashed with its contents staining the desk top and spattered down the side. A goblet was overturned. The dinner plate had skidded over the polished top when the inert body had struck it and flung the dishes helter skelter. But the big desk top had been large enough to keep the disturbed china from falling off.

Beau Quicksilver jerked up suddenly. His gray eyes narrowed. With a nervous gesture he brought out his platinum cigarette case. While he was striking a light his slitted eyes never left a single object which appeared half covered by an overturned plate.

Crackers and cheese lay on this under plate. And the cheese showed plainly the clearly defined outline of tooth prints.

But this was not all!

For the line of tooth marks there showed the peculiar outlines of a bicuspid and the first incisor—distinguishing characteristics anywhere.

For a moment the slim sleuth puffed away with scarcely the flicker of an eyelash. But within that subtle brain thoughts were swirling with lightning rapidity. One other thing he saw and filed away in his mind for important future action.

Then in a twinkling he brought out a pair of silk gloves and slid them on. He stooped and gently raised the fallen figure.

Cyrus Whitney had been a big man, heavily upholstered. Yet the lithe form of Beau Quicksilver raised the dead weight with no apparent effort. One began to sense beneath the supersmartly clad exterior the trained muscles of a Japanese athlete.

With expert, flashing movements Quicksilver continued his

rapid examination. Once he frowned suddenly. Then he replaced the body as it had been. With extraordinary care and dexterity he deposited the cheese within a little lacquered box in one of his pockets.

Then he strode swiftly to the door.

"Daniels," he rapped, "I am ready to ask questions. Have one of your men send the dead man's son, Ray Whitney, down to the library on this floor."

As Beau Quicksilver entered the room just named, he went directly to the fireplace. With a gesture of repugnance he dropped his silk gloves onto the smoldering blaze. They turned to tongues of flame. Next he produced a silk handkerchief and carefully wiped his hands. The handkerchief followed the silk gloves. With a dismissing shrug of his shoulders he turned to face Ray Whitney.

The money magnate's son was of the bulldog type—heavy featured, low browed, and bull necked. His shoulder breadth would have made him an admirable model for Atlas. Its girth was splendid. It suggested the far spaces and twelve-cylinder lungs.

"Were you in the house last night?" instantly lunged Beau Quicksilver.

Ray Whitney nodded somewhat curtly.

"All right. Give me all your movements up to the discovery of the crime."

The dead man's son shifted his big bulk, "Not much to tell. Came in about eleven, and went directly to my room. Didn't even see my father. He was an owl for late hours. Made it a daily habit to work or read until twelve thirty in his den. Was aroused by thundering knocks before daylight this morning. It was Stanley, the first man down. He'd noted the lights burning as they showed through under the door of the study. My father never left them on—fussy about useless extravagance. Stanley entered and discovered the dead body. He then alarmed the house. I called the police. That's all I know."

"Was your father in the habit of eating a late repast?"

"Always. We dine early. So every night Henry carried him a tray full of grub at twelve o'clock."

"Was it Henry's custom to return for clearing away the dishes after your father had retired?"

"No. Father was fond of old Henry. He made him go to bed after he had delivered the tray at midnight. The dishes were cleared away in the morning."

"Did your father like cheese?"

Ray Whitney stared at the foppish figure. A bit of a smile crept to his features, to be banished immediately.

"You've said it," he responded. "He was a nut on cheese. Insisted on it every night, both at dinner and with the midnight feed."

"Thanks—that's all."

"W-what do you make of the thing?" blurted out Whitney. "Will you ever be able to put your finger on the fellow that did it? Father's enemies were legion, you know. Might as well search for a particular leaf on a tree."

"I've got a scent," admitted Beau Quicksilver, "and it smells like cheese!"

With a blank expression on his heavy features, young Whitney went out.

The other inmates of the house merely corroborated the heir's statements. And each new bit of substantiating testimony simply strengthened the odor of the cheese clue. For one vital significant fact had stood out from the first. Moreover, it whispered of masterly cunning.

Beau Quicksilver's eyes were strangely bright as he sped away from the house. Subsequently the trailing of the truth was systematically begun.

CHAPTER III

AT FOUR O'CLOCK that afternoon Penn Markham, Quicksilver's assistant and confidant in crime, slipped excitedly into the apartment. He, too, was slight of build and approximately the mystery-master's height. His face also bore the brand of flashing intelligence.

He found Beau Quicksilver in the nattiest and completest of riding togs. The famous sleuth was evidently just in from a swift trot on Nemesis, his big black horse.

"Got it," rapped out Markham. "You couldn't miss it. And he didn't just recall them from his notes and charts!"

"Well," cut in Quicksilver, "spill it! What's the answer?"

"Parker Long is the man. He's known to be at swords' points with his victim."

Beau Quicksilver nodded. "I know the fellow. A born gambler. And a desperate plunger in the Street. A crack shot and a member of a number of sporty shooting clubs. A fellow known for his colossal nerve. The thing begins to fit in."

"To fit in!" echoed Penn Markham. "Why, it's done. It spells doom! It's like his fool presumption to gamble with discovery like that. The fellow always had a grim sense of humor. But this is irony—plus."

Beau Quicksilver said nothing. He merely stepped to the phone. Tersely he rapped out a number.

"Ah, is that you, Long? Quicksilver speaking. What do you say to a canter on the Speedway? I know you're strong for it in the late afternoon…. All right. Suits me perfectly. I'll be there on Nemesis quick enough to please you."

"Thunderation!" snorted Penn Markham. "Going to hobnob with him horseback and then break the glad news! You are a cool one. Going to drive him tandem up to police headquarters! Course he'll canter docilely ahead of you, and just joyously stretch out his wrists for the bracelets when you give the word!

Rotten form, Quixie. Guess that Everglades stunt you just pulled off has fagged you. You're riding to a fall, old man."

"Well, I'm not falling easy," retorted Beau Quicksilver—and was gone.

CHAPTER IV

IN A DECREPIT old farmhouse some miles away two men paced back and forth restlessly. The Falcon, slick jewel thief and crafty crime plotter, showed drawn lines about his mouth. And that bulldozing ruffian, Peter Scarlet, had faded a shade from his usual ruddy, overfed hue.

"If you hadn't been such a damned glutton, I'd feel easier," raged the Falcon. "Might have known you couldn't get by swell food—and toddy. I know you must have dropped something— left something behind, you filthy hog!"

For once Peter Scarlet didn't show fight. An uneasy expression filtered over his swinish features. He pulled at the lobe of his left ear, an unconscious habit he had when greatly disturbed.

"We've been here two nights now," went on the Falcon, nervously biting at his thin underlip in a futile effort to steady it. "And the very first night, in the dead of darkness, I heard a chawing and a gnawing like some devil ghost trying to tell me that you'd left tracks behind. Like the dead itself railing against respectable food gobbled up by a swine of a killer over the thing he'd made a corpse. All through the night I heard it gnawing— gnawing. And when I got up to look? Nothing! Not the sign of a mouse or a rat. After that first night I saw—you know whom. He swore there hadn't been a rat in the house for a year. Scarlet, if it isn't mice, what the hell is it?"

Uneasily Scarlet twitched at his ear lobes again. He attempted a superior smile. But the effort was a failure, as both men knew.

"Ask the devil! I don't know. I've piped it from the first. Didn't mind for a stretch. But when it kept up, hour after hour—well, nary a wink for mine. Eyes glued open—ears twitching to hear. And not a thing to put us wise as to what is the answer!"

"It's teeth chewing! Like yours chewed—that night," shivered the Falcon.

"Hell!" protested Peter Scarlet feebly.

But he continued to tug at his ear lobe. And his gross, florid face went a shade paler. "What's the use of standing here chewing it all over? If something's going to happen—well, let it! Come in and down a bite of grub. The stuff is getting cold on the table. Put it there myself before you let loose on the shaky chaw-chaw, you damned croaker!"

"There you go again!" snarled the Falcon. "I believe you would stuff yourself if you saw the gallows waiting for you."

Peter Scarlet shrugged. "Surest thing," he boasted. "Full belly makes a dead weight. Dead weight—taut noose."

"Oh, cut your poor jokes," flung back the Falcon, snuffing another shiver.

They entered a little room which they were using for a dining room. The table had been hastily set. Peter Scarlet flung himself heavily into a chair. His big, hairy hands grabbed at the food with bestial eagerness.

Suddenly he stopped. No morsel of food went to his lips. He pointed a spatulate finger at something on the table. His digit shook slightly, an index of sleepless hours— with some unseen thing gnawing away within him.

Jumpily the Falcon leaned forward. His eyes bulged from the sockets. His breath wheezed sharply.

For Peter Scarlet's blunt finger indicated a slice of bread with a huge bite missing. The marks of the teeth were plainly visible. The Falcon got up hastily. He shrank away from it as though it were the plague. His ghastly face twitched.

"I-it-it's a w-warning," he muttered hoarsely. "The h-house is h-haunted. H-he's come back to hound us!"

Peter Scarlet stared first at the shivery and fearful imprints, then at the Falcon's horrified countenance. The big criminal attempted to shrug his shoulders; but the effort ended in a shiver. Craftily he tried to conceal it. It would never do to let the Falcon see how craven fear was gnawing away in that spot where once good food and strong drink could silence anything.

The Falcon cried out shrilly: "Look! Look!"

He pointed a shaking hand at something which had fallen to the floor.

Peter Scarlet leaned over, pushing back his chair.

On the floor lay the napkin which the Falcon had dropped when he rose hastily. In a corner of the damask square something stared forth evilly, accusingly. It was the bloody print of teeth.

"God! There's blood on them," mumbled Scarlet to himself. "Whose blood?"

But the Falcon's every sense was strung tight. He heard the low words.

"Whose blood!" he blurted. "It's your blood!"

A wave of red seemed to flame from Peter Scarlet's pig eyes. The veins stood out on his bull neck. His great, hairy hands doubled into menacing fists. He advanced threateningly on the Falcon.

But the Falcon's eyes were not upon him. They seemed to be looking beyond him, quite unconscious of the red fury in his face. The Falcon's gaze was basilisk. His jaw dropped stupidly. He was like a man who sees a ghost—a terrible, avenging specter from which there is no escape.

Instantly the fear frozen there banished Scarlet's red choler. Instinctively he faced about, his gaze following the direction of the Falcon's horrified stare.

"H-he-he's h-here," blubbered the Falcon.

As Peter Scarlet looked, a huge cretonne-covered chair by the door began to move, slowly, surely.

For a moment the big criminal stood frozen to the spot.

Then he dashed forward. He flung the chair aside, yelling:

"Come out of there, you—"

But there was no one there. Only the floor sneered up at him—the floor and something else. For on it there lay a piece of cheese showing the marks of gory teeth.

Peter Scarlet staggered against the chair. The sweat dripped down his brutish features. His breath came quickly. Then—the door opened silently, swiftly. The Falcon screamed.

A smart, tweed-clad figure stepped in, nonchalantly unbuttoning a chamois glove. Beau Quicksilver stood there, his slim shoulders barely grazing the sturdy door closed behind him.

The sight of him slightly sobered the staggered Peter Scarlet. This was something he could understand. This was that damned dude detective—Beau Quicksilver. With a roar like an enraged bull, Peter Scarlet charged at the slight figure, his gross head lowered.

As his filthy breath almost fanned Quicksilver's features, the detective dodged and neatly tripped the great bulk. And Peter Scarlet, lunging with every ounce of rage in him, banged head first into the door. He dropped like a rotten apple from the sheer force of the impact and lay stunned.

The Falcon had crumpled up in a chair. They were beaten, and he knew it.

"G-God!" he moaned. "I felt it coming. Take me away from this place. It's damned—it's accursed. I'll spill the whole thing. Take me away! Lock me into a cell. It will be heaven beside this hell-hole—and the sound of teeth always gnawing-gnawing—"

His face was a blob of twitching whiteness.

Beau Quicksilver lunged to a window and beckoned.

CHAPTER V

"I'LL HAND IT to you, Quicksilver," admitted the chief. "You've pulled a humdinger. It's a big day when we get the goods on those two long-deserving blackguards. But I'm not clear on the details yet. I understand that a bite in a piece of cheese tipped you off. Careless play for a hardened crook like Scarlet!"

"Wrong," retorted Quicksilver. "The toothprints in the cheese were not made by Scarlet. We traced them from our enlarged photographs to the office of Dr. Lance Rainford, the swell West Side dentist. He didn't recall them merely from his notes and charts; he even had the original mold. For the fatal teeth belonged to a superb false set, a set cast from the mold made for Parker Long."

"I know Long—but where are the teeth leading us?"

"Not to the criminal—at first. You see, when I went horseback riding with Parker Long, he proved an ironclad alibi. He removed his set of false teeth before my very eyes. One of the damning teeth from that all-important set was missing. Luckily for him, he broke out that telltale tooth accidentally the night before the crime, when dining with Judge Rutledge. The jurist's substantiating word is gold.

"Long hadn't found time to go to his dentist for repairs. The marks on the fatal cheese were made from a duplicate set struck off from the original mold to incriminate Parker Long—a known enemy of Whitney. The dentist has confessed. He wouldn't talk at first. But when I told him that the Falcon and Peter Scarlet were in custody, and had blabbed the whole thing, he broke down and confessed."

"But how did you dope it out that Scarlet was the killer, that *he* planted the cheese with the indicative, damning prints, and that the Falcon's brain plotted the thing at the dentist's instigation to incriminate Parker Long?"

Beau Quicksilver smiled whimsically as he tenderly dusted his velvet hat.

"I called a *post-mortem* on the victim's stomach. It proved that Cyrus Whitney hadn't taken a bite before he fell dead amid the untouched food. *Yet the food had been devoured.* There is only one criminal who is glutton and ghoul enough to gorge himself over the body of the man he has just slain. That man is Peter

Scarlet. The rest was easy. Thanks to some clever haunt stuff, pulled off by the aid of a little electrical appliance, I produced the ghostly gnawings.

"It was a simple thing to do a bit of realistic chair-tipping by running a fine wire through a nail hole in the farmhouse floor to a covered chair leg. Nothing particularly clever about getting around without being seen with my men previously posted outside—I've been having the scoundrels shadowed, you know. The toothmarks salted away in the farmhouse were very effective. The most hardened crook fears to the point of maudlin terror what he cannot understand. So Conscience and Nemesis were my most valued allies."

"You can count ten, Quicksilver," grinned the chief. "I'm down all right. It's a knockout!"

AN EYE FOR AN EYE

WITH HARASSED, TWITCHING features, old Parkins conducted Dr. Cranston up the carpeted stairs.

"Dreadful thing! I can't believe it," the old servant kept muttering. "With him so hale and hearty! I can't believe it."

His voice broke in a moan. His dim old eyes were wet with tears. He kept swallowing in a vain effort to regain some vestige of control. For Parkins's devotion to the master of Maddox House was a country byword—as it had been for years.

Dr. Cranston's usual jovial features were clouded. Doubt and strained surprise looked forth from his deep-set eyes. He wet his lips before replying.

"I am as shocked as you are, Parkins. It strains belief. And it saddens me unspeakably. Yesterday I would have staked my professional reputation that Jonas Maddox was organically sound, and good for another healthy ten years at the minimum."

As servant and physician reached the top of the broad stairs a corridor door opened. A big man emerged. His face was solemn, his manner hushed. He stepped forward to greet the old family doctor.

"Sad business, Dr. Cranston. So sudden, so unexpected! It has rather floored us here, you know. Uncle Jonas never appeared better in his life than he did this evening. And now—"

The doctor jerked out his watch. "And now," he finished, "at 1 a.m., he lies dead in his bed."

"Gone without a moment's warning," wailed old Parkins

dolorously, wringing his hands. He looked shrunken and shaken. It was as though some one had slipped his anchor and he was drifting helplessly into an unknown, uncharted sea.

Almost curtly Dr. Cranston nodded toward a heavy closed door on the right-hand side of the corridor. A jagged break appeared in one of its panels.

"You had to force an entrance, I see."

Kendall Maddox nodded. "When Parkins knocked on the door at midnight to carry Uncle Jonas his customary nightcap, he received no response. This had never happened before. Parkins called loudly, thinking that his master dozed, although Uncle Jonas, as you know, has always been a confirmed night-hawk, reading till midnight. But Parkins's most stentorian cries could arouse no answer. Even with Uncle Jonas's deafness, he could not have failed to hear Parkins's repeated loud calls. The cries brought me out of my room. They also aroused my cousin Edith. She came out shivering and terrified."

"When did you last see your uncle alive?" demanded Dr. Cranston.

"Not since dinner. He retired directly afterward—as was his habit. I went to bed early myself."

"How did your uncle appear at dinnertime?"

Parkins cut in, his agitated spirit making him momentarily forget that he was still but the servant in the house: "I never saw him more chipper in my life, sir. He was in high spirits, laughing and joking in his big, hearty voice. He was always so considerate." Parkins moaned. "Being hard of hearing himself, he appreciated deafness even in an old servant."

A spasm of pain twitched at his features. But he went on: "That is the picture I want to remember of him—*alive*."

Gently, almost reverentially, Parkins opened the door of the death chamber. But he studiously kept his eyes away from the quiet figure in the bed. He was almost womanish in his dread of death.

With alert, quick step, Dr. Cranston entered, followed by

Kendall Maddox. He gave a hasty glance about the chamber which was half den, half sleeping room. The curtains were drawn. The electric lights still cast an amber glow over the ponderous interior.

Following his glance, Kendall Maddox offered: "W-w-we left the room j-just as we found it."

The doctor nodded in a preoccupied way. One could sense that words made little impression on his mind. His face was sad. For the dead man had been his friend.

His eyes went slowly to the silent figure that dominated the room. He saw the inert form bolstered up in bed by two pillows. Jonas Maddox seemed to be sleeping peacefully. One hand reposed beneath the coverlet. His heavy, tortoise-rimmed spectacles rested carelessly at one side. The other hand lay near a new detective story which remained pages down beside him.

The white face of the dead man was calm. No sign of pain rippled the still features. Except for the telltale pallor of the mien, no one would have dreamed that Jonas Maddox lay in his last sleep. It seemed as though the closed lips must open suddenly—that the familiar quizzical look of Jonas Maddox must once more surprise them.

Dr. Cranston stepped forward. Quietly he withdrew the coverlet and made accustomed, minute examinations. But the stalwart figure of Jonas Maddox told him nothing. The puffy purple indicative of apoplexy was not there. The limbs lay peacefully, naturally, unmarked by the faintest sign of paroxysm. There wasn't a scratch on the body—not even a pin-prick. Evidently Jonas Maddox had passed over the Great Divide while he slept.

Dr. Cranston straightened up. But the shadow was still heavy over his features. He paced back and forth on the polished floor. Once he paused by the reading table and frowned unseeingly at it. Then mechanically he resumed his restless walking.

"Well?" inquired Kendall Maddox at length.

His face was white and haggard. Seemingly the doctor's uncommunicative, studious air irked him. The muscles of his face twitched.

Sadly Dr. Cranston regarded the peaceful form of his old friend and patient.

"Heart trouble," he stated slowly. "Nothing else can explain it. It's a grim, subtle reaper. And it stalks where we least expect it. It has cut Jonas Maddox off at sixty—a man in his prime. Yet I swear on my professional honor that he was the last person I should have suspected of a defective heart. I'll make out a death certificate for heart disease. It must have been that. It's one of the deadliest, subtlest human evils to detect."

Again the doctor glanced hesitatingly around the room. Once more he stooped over the body of the dead man. He examined it again with painstaking, almost frenzied care. He shook his head.

"Death from natural causes," he reaffirmed. "There is not a hint of anything —wrong."

Still, his eyes clung persistently to the white, still face of Jonas Maddox.

"Well—I—think—that's all," he added haltingly, after another awkward pause. And in a brown study the doctor departed.

Within the mansion began the preparations for the proper interment of the master of Maddox House. But in the eyes of old Parkins there lurked an unforgettable sorrow—and a great, growing question.

CHAPTER II

DR. CRANSTON DRUMMED on his study desk. A slight, fashionably clad figure sat at a table near by, idly moving the pawns on a chessboard.

"Yes, the game fascinates me. It reminds me of—life," mused Beau Quicksilver, that "damned dude detective" to the criminal world.

One sensed an astute master in the slim, foppish figure. One admired the extreme fastidiousness and taste displayed in the ultrafashionable cut of the tweed suit. A magnificent fire opal gleamed like a spark of baleful red in the cravat. A duplicate stone was repeated in the setting of a ring worn on the little finger of the left hand. The opal might have stood for the methods of Quicksilver. For he, too, was like a dangerous, baleful eye, forever turned toward the dispersing of darkness and the dissipating of cryptic crime.

Dr. Cranston swiveled about in his chair. The indecision of the moment before had vanished from his manner. Grim determination shone there.

"Quicksilver, I know you're here to bag a few quail, among other quarry, while following that will-of-the-wisp inclination of yours. But I know mystery is the balm of life to you, the nectar of exhilaration. My friend, I am deeply perturbed. Something tells me that you ought to take the car and run over to Maddox House. You know I am just in from viewing the body of my old friend who died suddenly. I am on the point of making out a death certificate for heart failure. But—will you go over, Quicksilver? There is something the matter with me. I seem to need corroboration—a prop to lean on—before attesting to the cause of death on paper."

Beau Quicksilver turned from the chessboard.

"Of course I'll go, old fellow. Give me something to go on, first."

The doctor shifted.

"The facts are few. And they appear simple. There is not the ghost of evidence that anything is criminal."

Then he narrated the facts as he had found them.

"What is the personnel of the dead man's immediate family?" inquired Quicksilver.

"There is a niece, Edith Maddox—a slip of a girl of twenty. She is an art student at the League—with a future, they say. There is Courtney Maddox, a helpless paralytic nephew, you understand, and a dead weight physically. Been so for two years. Last there is Kendall Maddox, a young business man in the city—a second nephew."

"These three are the dead man's next of kin?"

"Yes. There are no other relatives."

"It interests me," announced Quicksilver decisively. "I'll go."

"Say that you are Dr. Beaumont, my consulting confrere from the city," interposed Dr. Cranston dubiously, "desiring a few more confirmatory facts on the death. The Maddoxes are a touchy lot—temperamental, you understand. Use discretion, my friend."

Beau Quicksilver grinned suddenly. The smile transformed his ordinarily rather ascetic face. It made him appear almost boyish. There was a whimsical twist to his lips.

"Discretion, O learned doctor, is the "watchword of snails and tabbycats, of hypocrites and sycophants. Strychnine is preferable to discretion. More respectable, you know. However, I'll not scrap the ethics of the medical profession. *Au revoir!*"

The door shut his slight, paradoxical figure from view.

Dr. Cranston stared for a moment thoughtfully at the place where Beau Quicksilver had been. Slowly the hint of a smile overspread his fine features. He soliloquized: "That chap is as much of a riddle as the mysteries he unravels. I never know where to find him next, either mentally or physically. He surely is—Quicksilver."

Later, Beau Quicksilver reentered the doctor's study. There were tired, almost petulant lines about his mouth. His shoulders sagged; he dropped limply into a chair. There was a querulous note in his voice, as though he had been unjustly cheated of a sprightly adventure.

"Nothing to whisper of foul play," he shrugged disgustedly. "Not a scratch. Nothing! Just a ham-and-eggs demise after all. And I thought I scented caviar! Bah!" He twirled his heavy ring idly. "I managed to talk to those whom I wanted to cross-question. Only the butler was missing. He seems to have disappeared. I wanted old Parkins's ideas," insisted Quicksilver peevishly. "Funny play, this sudden vanishing act of his."

Dr. Cranston's face showed immeasurable relief. "Any one would gather," he observed almost lightly, "that you feel badly treated, since you can find no evidence that violence has been done."

Again Beau Quicksilver shrugged. "Ordinary death is—ordinary death, to me."

CHAPTER III

THEY HAD BREAKFASTED and returned to the study when Dr. Cranston's new assistant knocked gently and entered.

"There's a bent and trembling old man asking to see you," he announced, addressing Beau Quicksilver. "I've told him that you're here on private business—loaded to the guards with weighty work. But for all his frailty he has a will of his own. He refuses to budge from the reception room. Declares that he must see the detectives—that it's vital. The old boy isn't cracked—that I'll wager. But he's carrying a heavy burden on his chest as I'm a judge. There is something about him that has got under my skin. Reminds me of a faithful, wounded dog, guarding something precious, you know."

Dr. Cranston looked up with marked surprise, saying: "He must be very appealing to pique your curiosity, Danton." For among the medicos in the city from which young Danton had just come he bore the appellation of "the Icicle."

Beau Quicksilver made an imperceptible gesture at Dr. Cranston. Turning to Danton, he smiled whimsically—almost joyously.

"Ah," he exclaimed, "so you've made yourself attorney for the defense! Did the mysterious, appealing and aged stranger give any name?"

"He did. Says he's Parkins, the old servant of the recently deceased master of Maddox House."

"Have Parkins in, Danton," said Beau Quicksilver crisply. "I'll hear what he has to say."

The slim detective appeared another person. Animation electrified his features.

"Shall I leave you?" suggested Dr. Cranston.

Quicksilver nodded. "Some of my questions would embarrass him with you here."

Without a word Dr. Cranston opened the door of the connecting room and closed it carefully behind him.

His exit was followed by the entrance of the faltering, trembling figure of the old man. Parkins's eyes were rimmed with red, his features sharp and sunken. He seemed on the point of collapse.

With gentle concern Beau Quicksilver rolled forward a heavily upholstered, comfortable chair. Parkins sank into it gratefully. His wrinkled fingers plucked nervously at the brim of his hat. He seemed to have difficulty in committing his mission to words.

"How can I help you?" inquired Quicksilver quietly.

"Will you?" flashed back the old man in a quavering voice. Dawning hope lighted his faded eyes. Some of the trembling left him.

"Most certainly, if whatever is troubling you interests me."

Still fumbling with his hat brim, Parkins covertly studied the keen-faced, alert-eyed man before him. Apparently satisfied with his scrutiny, he cleared his throat.

"I've heard about you, sir," he announced eagerly. "I know what you can do. That's why I have come to you."

"Yes?" Quicksilver helped him.

"You—you've heard of the sudden death of my master, Jonas Maddox?"

The detective nodded.

The old man's voice gathered strength. "There is something very wrong at Maddox House, sir. I can feel it in these old bones of mine. *My master never died of natural causes.* Dr. Cranston has made a fearful blunder."

Steadily Beau Quicksilver regarded him. "Why do you believe this? Surely you know Cranston's ability. He's one of the ablest men of his profession. He's also a toxicologist of note—a specialist in poisons, you know. You are hinting at foul play. Have you any evidence to substantiate this ugly suspicion?"

Pathetically Parkins watched him. "Not a jot of evidence, sir—except what I feel."

"It's natural for you to be shocked," went on Beau Quicksilver. "But surely if there were a scintilla of evidence that anything was wrong, Dr. Cranston would have noted it—it would have been seen."

Parkins shrugged his wizened shoulders. "Dr. Cranston is only human. The best and ablest of men slip up sometimes. Please don't laugh, sir. But the first thing that set me thinking was the door into—*his* room. We had to break it open, you know."

"Was it bolted on the inside?"

"No, sir, spring-locked."

"Well?"

"Sir, my master never locked his door at night. Never, sir, in all the long years I've served him. Besides, he knew that I would rap at midnight with his drink, sir. He always called out: 'Come in.' Then I would open the door and enter. Mr. Maddox never liked to leave his chair or his bed when he was deep in some new mystery, sir. The door's the thing that set me to thinking, sir. It was just as though some one in a desperate hurry forgot to slip off the catch and leave it unlocked as usual."

Absently Beau Quicksilver looked beyond the sad face and questioning eyes of the faithful servant.

"It's an interesting point," he granted. "Did Mr. Maddox leave a will?"

"No, sir. He told me if he ever made one I should witness it," proudly.

"Who inherits his vast property?"

"Mr. Courtney, Mr. Kendall, and Miss Edith, his two nephews and his niece—his only relatives, sir."

"When does the funeral occur?"

"Day after to-morrow, sir."

"Any further investigations on my part at this late hour might be awkward in the face of Dr. Cranston's death certificate," suggested Quicksilver.

"We can manage it, sir," rejoined Parkins eagerly. "I had it all thought out when I tried to find you in the city and was told you were here. Mr. Kendall went to the city before breakfast for the day on important, unexpected business. Mr. Courtney is helplessly confined to his room. Miss Edith is prostrated in her own. The servants won't count. I'll manage them. But I want you to examine—the b-body. I can't say for what, sir. But I think that you may see something which escaped Dr. Cranston. Until you are unable to find anything I shall not rest easy, sir."

"That locked door puts a different complexion on the matter," confessed Quicksilver, as though arguing with himself. "I'll just tell Dr. Cranston that I'm going out for a bit."

He left the room.

Parkins was aroused from his reverie by a loud knock at the door through which he had recently come. The door opened unceremoniously. A pompous, red-faced stranger entered. Prosperity and physical well-being were written over his correct, well-made clothes—his glossy silk hat.

"I've an appointment with Dr. Cranston," his voice boomed. "Dammit, sir, I can't keep waiting forever. Time is money, sir, with stocks sky-rocketing and breaking hourly."

He paused puffily, and stared over his gold-rimmed glasses with their heavy silk cord.

Parkins got up. "Sorry, sir," he said, deprecatingly. "Dr. Cranston isn't here—"

"Not here!" roared the pompous newcomer. "Well, I like his nerve! Tell him at once, sir, that Mr. Bartholomew Travers Mayflower is here."

Parkins looked helplessly about him. Then—

A merry, boyish laugh sounded. "Good old Parkins," said Beau Quicksilver's voice. "You're a flattering audience. Sorry to have caused you a moment's embarrassment. The new rig is necessary. Call me Mayflower for the present."

Shortly the pseudo Quicksilver, accompanied by old Parkins, was speeding away in a powerful roadster to Maddox House.

CHAPTER IV

AS PARKINS CONDUCTED the disguised detective up the broad stairs, Beau Quicksilver's keen glance noted everything. To the casual observer, however, he seemed a bored individual—plainly uninterested in his surroundings.

Presently they paused before the room with the drawn shades where the body of Jonas Maddox lay.

Parkins hovered outside. "I'll remain on guard, sir," he declared.

This was more from his desire not to enter than from the possibility of some awkward, unexpected interruption. Death hung heavy over Maddox House. The air seemed narcotized with sadness and the stunning suddenness with which disaster had fallen there.

Beau Quicksilver entered and closed the door. For some time he stood deep in thought, rigidly immobile. Then he approached the body of Jonas Maddox.

From a black leather bag he brought out for the second time a high-powered bulb with a length of cord. After attaching it, he redirected the powerful light upon the still figure. For a moment he stood as motionless as the form of the dead man lying there. Then a flash like unseen lightning gleamed from the detective's eye. The uncanny brilliance in Beau Quicksilver's orbs made the famous Kohinoor diamond look like a lump of charcoal by contrast.

Later when he emerged, bag in hand, Parkins looked up with startled, keen eyes. There was an odd expression on the detective's disguised features. His mouth was shut grimly—his jaw squared.

Beau Quicksilver held up a restraining hand. "I want to talk to Courtney Maddox and Miss Edith," he announced. "It might be better for you to resume your duties. I want to proceed without casting any suspicion as to my true identity."

"W-what shall I say to them, sir?"

"Tell them I'm an old friend of their late uncle arriving for the expression of sympathy. I'll phrase my questions carefully without revealing where they are leading."

Obediently Parkins knocked on the paralytic's door.

As he saw Beau Quicksilver's broadcloth back disappear within he went stumbling down the corridor.

"I knew it, I knew it," he kept moaning. "Oh, the poor master! Cut off before his time! Done to death by the arch deviltry of a fiend! I knew it, I knew it!"

Some time later Beau Quicksilver was ushered out a side door by Parkins.

"I'm driving directly back to Dr. Cranston's," he told the old servant in a cautious voice.

Soon the physician and Beau Quicksilver were in sober conference. Darker and darker grew the doctor's face. Horror stared from his eyes.

"A fearful thing, Quicksilver. I-I— can't believe it."

"Go back and see for yourself," rapped out Quicksilver. "The death certificate must be recalled. A fearful crime has almost been covered by it—a subtle, diabolical murder, worthy of the hypothetical master criminal. Meantime, I have much to do."

CHAPTER V

"**DR. CRANSTON AND** his medical friend wish to see you in the library, Mr. Kendall, sir," announced Parkins, shakingly, some time later.

"What does Cranston want?" demanded Kendall, pulling off his coat. "This is a funny time to come into a house of mourning."

"He didn't tell me, sir," answered Parkins mechanically, and turned away.

"We've been waiting for you," declared Dr. Cranston without preamble, as Kendall Maddox entered the room. "Dr. Beaumont and I have been in further consultation over your uncle's death."

"Thought that was all settled," remarked Kendall Maddox, flinging himself into a chair.

The doctor paced back and forth nervously. Beau Quicksilver lounged easily in a seat by a table.

"Dr. Beaumont here has another theory regarding the real cause of death," stated Cranston.

Maddox said nothing. His eyes went to the quiet figure at the table. He noted approvingly the nobby clothes. He was a bit of a dresser himself. But he was a big fellow, and in his eyes lurked all the contempt of the muscular giant for a lightweight specimen of the *genus homo*.

"Yes," agreed Beau Quicksilver, his inscrutable eyes on Kendall Maddox's face. "Your uncle did not die from any form of heart disease."

"How did he die, then?" asked Kendall Maddox in deep surprise.

"Not from natural causes," declared Beau Quicksilver. *"Jonas Maddox was murdered."*

Kendall Maddox stared evenly at the man before him.

"How do you know?" he asked languidly.

"I'll tell you how. *Rigor mortis* tattled on the murder. It was the accuser, inexorably pointing out that murder had been done."

"But," objected Kendall Maddox, "Uncle Jonas's body was unscratched. There wasn't a mark on it to whisper of anything wrong."

"True. But that diagnosis was made because investigations had been conducted *before rigor mortis set in.* Jonas Maddox's murderer reckoned without that. With a powerful nitrogen bulb I examined the body when cold in death. By the aid of the light I was struck with one thing—the appearance of your late uncle's right eye. I found that, with the contraction of the muscles in death—with the coming of *rigor mortis*—the right eye protruded slightly more than the left. I learned why. Jonas Maddox was a proud man—vain of his personal appearance. When abroad some months ago a serious infection of the right eye made its removal imperative. The operation was done by a great French oculist. A wonderful glass eye was made and set into the empty socket. To make detection even more impossible Jonas Maddox was outfitted with a particular kind of spectacles carrying heavy tortoise rims. No one knew of the existence of this false eye—except one person. This was the murderer who plotted and planned accordingly. For Jonas Maddox was stabbed to the brain through the right eye socket when the glass eye had been temporarily removed. One of Miss Edith's etching needles—fine and keen-pointed—could have done the deed. Death was instantaneous and painless. The dead man's dinner coffee had been drugged with a slow-working but powerful narcotic. An analysis of a fresh coffee stain on the tablecloth confirms this fact. Internal cerebral hemorrhage—a clot on the brain—told nothing. It was short work for the murderer to conceal the crime by replacing the glass eye in the sightless socket. Nor was there a single clue to whisper the truth until, cold in death, the real eye receded slightly—flattened into the head—while the glass eye could not do this."

Kendall Maddox was staring intently at Quicksilver.

Coolly the detective shot out: *"Kendall Maddox, you killed your uncle!* You're the only person capable of committing such a crime. The house is equipped with a modern, highly efficient burglar-proof system. This was not tampered with on the night of the crime. So no outsider could have entered. You committed the deed on the night when all the servants but deaf and near-sighted old Parkins had their night off. So within the house were only a helpless paralytic, a sensitive girl who would cry at the sight of a hurt kitten, a near-sighted, devoted old servant—*and you.*"

Kendall Maddox shrugged insolently. "The vaporings of a madman! Without a shred of proof! You've had a bad nightmare—but it is high time you woke up!"

Languidly Beau Quicksilver raised a hand. From it dangled an expensive imported cigarette.

"I am not finished. On the under side of the glass eye is microscopically etched the famous oculist's name and address. Modern science has annihilated distance, fortunately for justice. From Paris I learned that you accompanied your uncle for the eye operation—that you, alone with the specialist, had been sworn to secrecy concerning the existence of the glass eye."

Kendall Maddox rose calmly. "Might as well be killed for a sheep as a lamb," he remarked coolly. "The game is up. It meant imprisonment for me unless I got my inheritance money in a hurry. Uncle had refused to give me the necessary currency. I thought I had the thing worked out beyond discovery. I never reckoned with *rigor mortis,* a tattling eye, and you."

THE CLAWS OF THE WEASEL

IN THE SWAGGEREST of evening attire Beau Quicksilver slipped into his seat in the dress circle. The orchestra sounded the introductory prelude to the famous opera with its mysterious minor notes. Would they, too, that very evening sound for him some weird new prelude, not to a masterpiece of melody, but to some masterpiece of criminal cunning?

The slim figure deposited its smart high hat carefully under the seat and necked off a few invisible notes from the immaculate gloves—gloves which would never be worn but once. As Beau Quicksilver languidly leaned back, one of his legs protruded a bit beyond his aisle seat. One wondered slightly to note patent leather shoes a shade less modish than the rest of the ultra-smart garb.

Across the aisle a cub reporter, with a sprouting toothbrush on his upper lip, tipped off his suburban companion. "D'you lamp that swell across the aisle—the fashion plate that just breezed in? Well, that's Beau Quicksilver, the dude detective. And you can take it from yours knowingly that he's a regular king pin, a famished fire-eater for cryptic crime. Slick! Well, mercury has nothing on him, since he's *it*. He's pulled more big cases in a year than all the flatfoots together. And fussy! Oh, my! Won't even nibble at a regular killing. Gotta have something outre—an out-and-out enigma with all the flossy frills. Otherwise, 'Nothing to it,' says he. 'Give it to some prep school kids to work out in algebra! It's the real goods or nothing!' Say," went on the write-up man, "remember that vanishing Hindu stunt he pulled a month ago? Well, that's A, B, C compared to some of the crimes he's seen to a finish. Little? Yes, but, oh, my! There's not a yegg in crookdom that can lay a digit on him. He just runs through their fingers—"

Over the way, Beau Quicksilver leaned back fagged, utterly fatigued. It had been a momentous week. Behind his half shut, aching lids, the mysterious magic of the melody filtered soothingly. Through his slitted eyes he languidly noted the stirrings of the velvet draperies in box A in the first tier next the stage.

With great unction the usher was showing in a regal dowager dame and a slender, sylphlike girl. The elderly woman would indeed have been a notable figure anywhere. Masses of silver hair were cunningly coiled above the haughty mien. The roseate hue of health and good living was cleverly blended with rouge over her high-bred features. She held a jeweled lorgnette constantly to her languid eyes. Her lavender evening gown sparkled with crystal and beading.

The young girl with her slipped with elfin grace into her seat by the rail of the box. Her dainty dress, the faintest apricot in shade, made her appear more like a flower swaying to the urge of the music than the slip of the debutante she seemed.

A pompous, fidgety man next to Quicksilver addressed his companion:

"Those two there," he was announcing in a stage whisper, "the woman in lavender and, the girl in pink. That's Mrs. Wellington Denmore Rutherford—wife of the copper king, you know. And the girl is her niece, Betty Rutherford, just come on for a season here. Big money there—and power, too—"

The awed and adulatory accents of the gentleman gossip next to Quicksilver merely verified the growing thought in the detective's mind. He had known instantly that the face of the woman in lavender had seemed familiar. He recalled seeing Mrs. Rutherford's photograph many times in the society columns.

A few moments later an usher entered box A hastily. He bent over the lady deferentially, but jerkily. His nervousness must be apparent anywhere in the house. Beau Quicksilver raised his glasses to the white blotch of the usher's face framed against the gray velvet hangings. He was an adept at lip-reading.

He saw the usher's twitching mouth frame itself into these words: "A dreadful thing, Mrs. Rutherford. Just had a message. Mr. Rutherford has been—" At this moment the agitated usher nervously shifted his position to a side posture. His moving lips were no longer visible to the dapper figure in the dress circle.

Hastily the woman in lavender, followed by her niece, left the box. Mrs. Rutherford's haughty, assured air was gone. She held her handkerchief before her blanched features. And the girl, not yet ossified by the pose and the aplomb of society, stumbled along in the rear of her aunt, making unconscious, pathetic little dabs at her great, gray eyes.

The two had hardly disappeared when an usher touched Beau Quicksilver on the arm. As the minor motif was reiterated by the throbbing violins, the detective reached out his hand for the card which the attendant was proffering.

On one side the card was engraved with the name:

MRS. WELLINGTON DENMORE RUTHERFORD

Flipping it over Beau Quicksilver read the message, cupped by his hand:

Please come to my car at the curb before the opera house. A dreadful thing has happened. I need your advice. Please.
HONORIA RUTHERFORD.

Mechanically Beau Quicksilver reached for his opera hat. He shot it under his arm and strode out behind the usher just as the lights blinked dark and the curtain rolled up. Yet he did not begrudge the loss of an operatic evening. The melody of mystery had again sounded its prelude. And for him cryptic crime was a symphony which acted as a tonic on his every nerve.

A huge lavender limousine with an imposing monogram on the door was drawn up at the curb just beyond the main entrance to the opera house. A lavender-liveried chauffeur touched his cap and alertly opened the door. He gently and deferentially shut it after Beau Quicksilver's figure.

The two women leaned back limply against the upholstery. Mrs. Rutherford was sobbing now, her social mask dropped when away from the curious, appraising eyes of the crowd. Her head was bowed. And her handkerchief, like herself, had shrunk to a limp mass. Grief is a leveler. And evidently the proud woman before him had her limitations.

As for the girl, some of her control seemed to have returned. She sat rigidly, her tiny hands tightly gripped in her lap. She had drawn a costly evening wrap close over her slim shoulders. And she sat hunched into it, a forlorn little picture, despite the elegance of her apparel. She reminded Quicksilver of a sleek, well-fed kitten which has suddenly become surrounded by unfamiliar, terrifying things. Tragedy was an ugly stranger—and an unwelcome one.

The detective bowed low, his sleek, dark head dimly outlined in the soft, indirect lighting of the car.

"How can I serve you, madam?" he asked quietly.

"Please be seated," came in muffled accents from behind Honoria Rutherford's handkerchief.

She reached to the side of the car, extracted a bottle of smelling salts and sniffed at them as though to draw solace and strength for the coming ordeal.

"I—I j-just h-had a m-m-message—which the usher brought to my box—that Mr. Rutherford h-has been found s-stabbed to d-death in the seat of his roadster in the garage. T-they just found him."

Beau Quicksilver looked out of the window. A mental image of the violently slain copper magnate filmed across his mind. He saw the stern, frowning face of Rutherford with its thin lips and bulldozing jaw. It was a domineering face as well as a ruthless one. Its lineaments plainly bespoke a merciless nature, one which must, perforce, be beset by many enemies. A violent death for Rutherford did not surprise Quicksilver. It merely corroborated his estimate of the man.

"Have you any other particulars?" he asked quietly.

"N-no." The sob had returned to her voice. "O-only I—I've been fearing it would come."

"And why?" asked the detective, toying with a heavy set ring on the little finger of his left hand.

"H-he's been threatened with his l-life."

"Through anonymous, blackmailing letters?"

"N-no. Ugly messages o-over the phone and by telegram."

"Of what nature?"

"They just said that he could expect to d-die in a hurry—or something like that."

"Did Mr. Rutherford take no precautions against sudden murder?"

"He w-wouldn't. J-just laughed and swore at them. Said he'd like to see them g-get him. He obtained a permit to carry a revolver for self-protection. Won't you come home with us, p-please? P-price is no object. I—I don't want those bungling policemen stamping about and—seeing nothing. They will never get the answer. Won't you come, please?"

The girl, too, gazed at him appealingly, her eyes dry but feverishly bright. Already purple shadows appeared under them. And the oval face looked wan and white.

"I will come, madam," answered Beau Quicksilver.

"Oh, thank you," sobbed Mrs. Rutherford.

Then she took down the speaking tube. To the waiting chauffeur she said: "H-home, please, Flanders."

The lavender limousine started. Soon it was under smooth but rapid momentum. It swirled away from the bright lights on to the broad boulevard. Its eight cylinders seemed rhythmically to repeat the whispering motif from the opera its occupants had just left.

CHAPTER II

THE LIMOUSINE HAD swept on in silence for some moments. They had now left the boulevard for the pike which ran to the suburb in which the imposing Rutherford estate sprawled over some acres. It was one of the newer residential districts with sparse, snobbish mansions perched here and there at indifferent intervals.

When the car passed under one of the infrequent arc lights Mrs. Rutherford begged: "Won't you please draw the shades by you? The light hurts my eyes."

As Beau Quicksilver courteously complied the girl, too, leaned forward and thoughtfully pulled down her shades.

"Thank you," murmured the broken woman. "I feel as though I could scream at nothing."

Quicksilver leaned back against the cushions. He crossed one leg over the other. His patent leather shoes gleamed dully, like some anomaly in the luxuriously correct interior of the limousine.

Suddenly Honoria Rutherford sat up. She made a quick

gesture. An ugly, snouty revolver was gripped in her right hand in a very businesslike way. Gone was her grief with its accompaniment of sham sobs.

"Put 'em up, you damned dude!" a harsh, nasal voice demanded.

"Make it quick, you tailor's bandbox!" jeered the pseudo-niece, showing the duplicate of the thirty-two in her own small hand.

Smothering a yawn Beau Quicksilver's hands went resignedly over his head. His crossed leg swayed slightly, as though he still heard the rhythm of the music. Or was it merely from the motion of the law-breaking car?

"Played you for a sucker, didn't we?" sneered the big woman. "Fell hard, didn't you? Bolted the whole frame-up, line, hook and sinker. You're a hell of a detective—you are."

Beau Quicksilver now recognized the raucous twang of the woman opposite him. Admiration colored his choler, his irascibility at his gullible stupidity. For the woman before him, wonderfully made up to resemble Mrs. Rutherford, could be no other than Lady Mag, a notorious woman crook. She had won the sobriquet from her ability to play high-class, fashionable roles as to the manner born. It was hinted that she was a woman of education, had belonged to a decent family—before the specious lure of crime had claimed her. And Lady Mag was a wizard at make-up—as well as a mimic. She had not belied her reputation. As for the girl? Some new tool probably, an able second to foil Lady Mag's dowager parts when necessary. Beau Quicksilver ground his teeth.

Lady Mag saw the motion and laughed harshly.

"Little toy detective, eh, what? Wound up wrong this time! Yes? Listens hateful, Buster Beau! Grind your teeth all you want to, you boob! Put an edge on them. Bite yourself. For you won't bite us any longer. We're going to draw your teeth!"

"If you have handcuffs along," suggested Quicksilver evenly, "I'd recommend that you manacle my hands behind me. My wrists are becoming tired with this novel uplift movement you've staged." He stifled a yawn. "One of you can cover me while the other snaps on the bracelets."

"Nothing doing," snapped Lady Mag scornfully. "We weren't born yesterday. Don't quite run in the flapper class. Get me?"

Beau Quicksilver shrugged. "As you please."

For a while only the roar of the engine swirling along at breakneck speed enlivened the interior.

Then: Beau Quicksilver merely uncrossed his leg and slid it down toward the other high-shod foot.

There was an odd sound. With it Quicksilver bent over with monkeyfied agility. He leaned against his silk hat beside him.

There was a little gasp—two of them. The dim-lighted interior was instantly shrouded with a thick, gray mist which hid the two women from him like some odd trick of legerdemain. But over his face appeared a highly efficient, up-to-date, collapsible gas mask which he had quickly removed from the inside of his silk hat.

The bodies of his two captors lay temporarily unconscious on the cushions opposite him. Their revolvers were still tightly gripped in their fingers.

Humming a snatch of the motif from the opera, Beau Quicksilver quickly freed their fingers from the revolvers. He put the weapons carelessly in his pockets, then reached for the door of the gas-filled interior.

As he did so the car came to an abrupt halt and he was flung rudely against the upholstery.

The limousine door opened. The liveried chauffeur stood there posing a forty-four. Evidently Lady Mag had pressed a warning buzzer to the driver's seat before the gas completely gripped her.

The fumes of the gas billowed out. But the purifying oxygen outside rendered the chauffeur temporarily immune from the effects of it.

"Come out of there, you rat!" he snarled, throwing a circle

of light from a flash full on Beau Quicksilver. "Step lively now, or I'll drill your ruffled shirt-front—make you a messy job for the undertaker. Get a move on!"

Sticking the flash in his pocket the chauffeur covered his nostrils with his handkerchief.

As Quicksilver automatically obeyed, the faked Flanders slammed the door shut on the deadening fumes. He breathed heavily for a bit, but kept his pistol leveled at the detective. They had driven off the main pike upon a narrow, thickly wooded dirt road. The lights of the car had been switched off.

"Now, keep 'em up," growled the chauffeur, fully recovered from the insidious effects of the gas. "Careful now while I frisk you, you damned dirty dick!"

In a twinkling he relieved Beau Quicksilver of the guns which the detective had taken from the two unconscious women.

"Where the hell did you get that gas? Did you have it parked on you? Sloppy work for Lady Mag and the Kid to let you spring that kind of a gag! Hell, that's like a couple of women! Now," continued the pseudo-chauffeur briskly, "in you go again! Try some of your own medicine!"

He yanked the gas mask from Quicksilver's face and slipped the protecting shield over his own features. Mockingly he opened the door. Roughly he shoved Beau Quicksilver onto the upholstered seat.

A suffocating blanket seemed to engulf the detective. It closed about him subtly, insidiously. It touched his respiratory organs and turned them *nil*. But, from afar off, through his benumbed senses, he could still seem to hear the poignant, sobbing note of a violin singing out the music of the world-renowned opera. And despite the darkness which was closing in upon him, his soul was filled with ecstasy at the note of beauteous mystery concealed in the melody.

CHAPTER III

WHEN BEAU QUICKSILVER recovered consciousness gray dawn was seeping through the windows into his prison. Weakly he sat up to find himself on a comfortable couch in a luxuriously furnished room which appeared like some rich man's study. There were well-filled bookcases about; handsomely upholstered furniture, a desk with complete equipment for writing, and a big, Jacobean library table. But the two windows did not suggest a rich man's idle hour room, for they were heavily barred. Moreover, the apartment was on the third floor. It overlooked a melancholy landscape—a gray, apologizing sky and frowning, thick woods. There was one door in the room—a thoroughly efficient and heavily hinged affair. The place made an admirable prison.

Beau Quicksilver got to his feet and fished about in his pockets. Their contents had not been disturbed. With the assurance that he concealed no other weapons, his captors had left him his harmless accessories. He brought out a silver cigarette case and lighted a weed.

He paced toward the bookcase. He smiled whimsically, admiringly. He had not been wrong. The criminal circle which had been operating for so many weeks *was* directed by a superior intelligence. He had believed it before. Now the idea assumed reality. The books told him much. Among those present appeared Balzac, Voltaire, De Maupassant. There were also Lombroso, Havelock Ellis and some of the lesser students of crime. A leather-bound set of Browning democratically rubbed elbows with Bliss Carman and Robert W. Service.

A smile of pleasure curved Beau Quicksilver's rather pale lips. So this was the lair of the elusive master criminal who had been balking him and the department for so many weeks. Admiringly he gazed about him. Smilingly he recalled the clever plan by which he had been spirited to the spot.

Why hadn't they killed him and had it over with? Why the cat-and-mouse play? Had some lingering form of death been reserved for him? Or was the master still away—that carnivorous, crafty mind whom they had come to call the Weasel?

A key sounded in the door. The heavy barriers swung open. The slight, wide-eyed girl of the night's unpleasant experience stood there. She shut the door behind her and stood with her back against it.

"You're a sick looking dude," she sneered.

"Sorry I can't return the compliment," he answered gallantly, strolling to a window and looking out.

"Say, do you know what you're in for?" she demanded.

"An unpleasant morning," he retorted, "accompanied by rain, if I'm a weather prognosticator."

"An unpleasant morning, accompanied by—a little lead pellet equipped with a silencer," she flung back. "He should be here now almost any time. He made us swear to keep you for his own special attention," she added meaningly. "He's fond of shooting, you understand—of hunting down sly, dangerous quarry."

"Lucky he doesn't get mixed up in his own gun then," answered Quicksilver, snuffing his cigarette and throwing it into the waste basket. "Pardon the weed, I'd forgotten it."

He sat down limply on the edge of the couch. His braggadocio air seemed to desert him. His slight body shook with a shiver.

"Guess the weed made me sick," he confessed naively. "Or the gas—or what's coming to me."

He smiled in a sickly way. His face was white. His features worked. Fear stared from his eyes. The cocky bravado of a former moment had fallen away.

The girl at the door watched him. A sneer commingled with another emotion rippled over her face.

"Not quite so perky as you were, eh, what? Throwing a shiver already. Most of them do when they see death blinking at 'em."

Beau Quicksilver seemed unconscious of her gibes. He appeared wrapped up in his own misery and the doom which was closing in upon him. His shoulders shook slightly. He turned his head away so that the girl might not see his face.

But she stepped cattishly to one side of the door. And then she saw. There were tears in the famous dick's eyes. He was biting his trembling lips. One of his hands edged for his handkerchief.

She smiled in a superior way and shrugged her shoulders.

He turned toward her. Misery was written over his woebegone features.

"I suppose you think I am a craven and a coward. B-but I'm not crying for myself. It's for Penn, my pal. I promised him that I'd never pass over without sending him a line—a few farewell words, you know." His voice broke. "I wouldn't mind being bumped off if I could just say good-by as I promised. I've never broken my word."

The woman straightened up. Some of the sneer left her face. Somewhere within her calloused, crime-soaked interior his words struck a responsive chord. Among those of the underworld who were her regrettable associates the Kid, too, was known never to break her word. Promises were a fetish with her. She began to sense the misery of the figure before her.

"Cut the cry-baby stuff! Now, how did you dope it out to get a message to him? Tell me that!"

"Well," he replied disconsolately, "I figured that some one here might take down one for me."

Craftily she backed away from the idea.

"Playing to send an S.O.S. in code, are you? Ring off—line busy! Nothing doing!"

"You mistake my meaning," answered Beau Quicksilver stiffly, "I don't set a bunch like you down for fools. Naturally, you wouldn't be silly enough to write docilely at my dictation!"

"What's the idea, then? Get to it without the frills."

"There's pen and paper on the table. Sit down at the desk

and write a few lines as you'd write to a pal if you're sending a last message."

With a frown between her keen eyes the Kid considered. "Sounds twenty-two carat—and yet—"

After a minute she went on: "Well, I'll put it up to Wildcat. He's strong on keeping his word—like me."

The door clicked behind her.

With three paces Quicksilver reached the desk. His slim fingers went to his pocket. Then they capped into the desk drawer, and away again.

He returned to his forlorn position by the window.

Shortly a newcomer unlocked the door and entered. A slim, hawk-eyed fellow stood there, of approximately Beau Quicksilver's build and height. One hand was in his pocket where an automatic bulged unmistakably.

"Well, now, what's the dope?" he rapped out. "What's this steer on some farewell stuff the Kid's been mouthing? Get it out in a hurry for he'll be here any time. And then there'll be something doing," he added.

Beau Quicksilver repeated his forlorn request as he had tremblingly stated it to the Kid. "Sit down at the desk there. Take your pen, your ink and paper and write a decent note to Penn Markham—you've heard of him."

Craftily the Wildcat considered. "Nix," he said, "on the desk paper and ink there. That listens phony. We're taking no chances on you. Understand? But I brought up a sheet of paper from downstairs—and my own fountain pen. I'll spin a few words. A guy wouldn't want to pass in his checks and break his promise!"

As he seated himself he reconsidered. "But, say, how's the note going to get to him? We don't send any one of this gang into a trap! Get me? What's the idea?"

"You're wise, all right," answered Beau Quicksilver admiringly. "I fancied you'd be. Just get one of your gang to slip out in one of the big cars to the city and drop the letter into a mail box—any mail box he chooses. Nothing shady about that, you see."

The Wildcat pondered. "That's all right," he decided. "Now shut up while I write a swan song in a hand that nobody 'll spot."

Through slitted lids Quicksilver watched him. Laboriously the fountain pen scratched across the self-provided sheet.

Then the Wildcat read the result:

> "Good-by, old top. They've got me this time. I shall pass in my checks pretty soon.
> > "Yours,
> > > "Beau Q."

"Fine!" approved Beau Quicksilver. "Couldn't be better. You're a fellow that's strong on his promises, too. Much obliged! One other little thing—I've got to get that letter to him in a hurry. He's booked for California this morning. We'll have to stick on stamps enough to make it special delivery."

Frowning, the crook thought again. "Oh, all right," he said. "That's that!"

Then the Wildcat blotted the letter, put it in the envelope he'd brought with him and sealed it. He reached for the desk drawer, and brought out six stamps. Beginning at one end, he licked them thoroughly.

A surprised expression clouded his features. The letter and the moist stamps fell limply from his hands. He attempted to get up. He made a weak gesture toward his bulging hip pocket. To no avail. He slumped back inertly into the chair.

Beau Quicksilver strode to the unconscious figure. Quickly he exchanged his disheveled evening dress for the loud, sporty clothing of the limp Wildcat. He pulled the checked cap off the slumped head and down over his own ears at a rakish angle. He hunched up the collar in a rowdyish way, ludicrously like the unprotesting dupe. Then he laid the careless crook in his own soiled evening clothes on the couch as though sunk in

deep slumber. Boldly he opened the door, locked it and pock-
eted the key.

He descended the stairs. The doped stamps he had substi-
tuted for the original ones would keep the Wildcat a dead factor
for some time.

"Well?" whispered the Kid cautiously from the unlighted
lower hall.

"It's all right," came the Wildcat's familiar drawl. "Going to
post it myself. Keep it dark if he gets here. Tell him I've got a
hunch on the bulls. Get me?"

"You've said it," she agreed, and went back down the corridor.

With a scornful roar a big car swept out of the garage. The
slim shoulders of Beau Quicksilver rocked with silent laughter.
But to any peering spectator they seemed merely to reflect the
careening movement of the motor.

Before that master criminal, the Weasel, returned to the
distant house, Beau Quicksilver and the police had already
taken captive its cornered inmates. So the crafty head of a
notorious criminal clique walked quite unsuspectingly into a
trap instead of to the swift and silent execution he had so painstakingly planned.

And it was Quicksilver himself, still clad as the Wildcat—
with a few more characteristic lines from a make-up box—who
opened the door and let the Weasel step into the drawn net.

Beau Quicksilver whistled an aria from the lost opera as he
donned tennis togs.

Then he answered Penn Markham, busy with the racket
stretchers: "Close call? Perhaps. But there is no sport in an easy
game. And I had several tricks up my sleeve, you know."

His eyes fell upon the discarded and very helpful patent
leather shoes. Penn Markham followed his glance.

"Nobby little invention of yours, Quixie! Gas shoes—double
shoes with a steel-enclosed space like a thermos bottle, equipped,
not with a vacuum, but with knockout gas. Clever little catch,
too, that will spill the gas with a kick of your foot."

Beau Quicksilver turned languidly to his discarded silk hat. It carried a double top where the collapsible gas mask had been concealed.

"Slovenly work"—he shrugged—"denting up a decent lid like this! Got to get a new one made!"

THE HAND OF THE HYENA

"**AMUSING LITTLE EPISTLE!** So gentle and solicitous for my health." Beau Quicksilver languidly tossed over the letter he had just received by special delivery.

The characters of the message were set down in ruddy red, of an insidious and exceedingly suggestive hue. The communication ran:

> YOU DAMNED DUDE:
> We are sending *this* letter in *red ink*. But we shall soon *write in your blood* to the gang the glad word that you've slipped your wind. We are going to get you, you dirty dick—you little dolled-up excuse of a tailor's dummy! *You can't shake us!* We've got *Jack Ketch* camping on your trail.
> We dare you to set foot outside your diggings this evening. We swear that if you put half a toe toward that carnival thing—*you're a goner.*
> THE HYENA.

Penn Markham, the noted detective's most intimate friend and sharer in his criminal exploits, studied the letter soberly.

"Funny move," he remarked, "putting you wise like this. With such a fly in your ear they can hardly expect you to leap for it. Naturally you won't budge with such a pleasant little reception committee awaiting you. Forewarned, you know—"

The splendid figure of Beau Quicksilver leaned forward in the great chair. The dude detective wore the costume he had most painstakingly designed for the carnival at the league that evening. It was already very dark outside. And Quicksilver momentarily expected his long, gray car to swerve up to the curb. For the motor, like its master, thrilled under the slightest acceleration of forthcoming cryptic adventure.

Beau Quicksilver was clad in the habiliments of the long ago. His satin doublet was of the richest scarlet. The crimson knee breeches gleamed with buckles set in brilliants. Buff hose ended in scarlet buckled shoes. And as was fitting for a dandy, a retainer in the court of Queen Elizabeth, Beau Quicksilver wore a high ruff at his throat almost touching his chin. At his side hung a sword in a marvelously chased scabbard. He might have been Robert Dudley, Earl of Leicester, as he sat there. Somehow the splendid raiment of bygone days seemed to become perfectly this modern knight of helpless law—of justice perpetually in distress.

"I should worry," smiled Beau Quicksilver disdainfully as he polished the tip of his scabbard with a lace kerchief. "Daring me to keep my engagement this evening because they know I make a fuss about such little things! Throwing a defy—a taunt to see if they judge me aright. Well, they do. For I shall attend the carnival in costume precisely as scheduled. *That* for their threats!" And he snapped his slim fingers.

A shadow fell over Penn Markham's fine face. "Quixie, old man," he worried ominously, "your decision is worthy of you. And I detest a coward. But aren't you rather overdoing the thing? Think what your loss would mean to the Criminal Investigation Department—to public safety. They're going to get you one of these nights, Quixie, old boy."

Again Quicksilver shrugged his satin shoulders. His gray eyes gleamed like the brilliants on the gay buckles. "They may get me for a few hours, Penn. But that's all. I tell you, old top, the mind is quicker than mere muscle. So I always intend to be two mental jumps ahead of the criminal's muscular 'rough stuff.' Can a ten-ton truck catch a weasel?"

But the shadow still hovered over Penn Markham's clean-cut

features. His further protestations against what he considered Beau Quicksilver's foolhardy quest were nipped by two blasts, followed by a short one, from the big-throated siren outside.

"Ah, there's the Greyhound," smiled Quicksilver animatedly, for so he had christened that long, lithe line of tempered steel.

Clicking his heels together the courtly figure made Penn Markham a sweeping bow.

"Au revoir," called back the slim form as it leaped to the door. "Don't bother about Jack Ketch. The hangman's noose is a relic of medieval monstrosity. While I may wear the habiliments of other days, I am mentally accoutered with an entirely up-to-date twentieth century wardrobe."

"Adieu!" rejoined Penn Markham.

And Beau Quicksilver's gallant figure vanished from sight.

But his associate's clouded eyes continued to scan the leering, blood-red lines which made up the threat of the Hyena. The symbols there took on the character of something evil—until they seemed to sneer at him in letters of blood—Quicksilver's blood.

CHAPTER II

OUT IN THE river varicolored lights blinked from the darkness with knowing red, green, or blue eyes. Hardly a star answered the winks from the stream. For the night was dark. No moon sailed overhead.

In a disreputable old boathouse on the right bank of the river a group of men waited expectantly. But their eager glances set evilly in their hardened, ruthless faces. They reminded one of the boa constrictor stalking an antelope and licking anticipatory chops with its quarry already in sight.

A big man with bullock shoulders and a bullet head addressed them. He might have been the living prototype of Mephistopheles, done on generous lines, so diabolical was his expression. He tugged at the end of a bulbous nose, a habit he had when pluming himself on some damnable achievement.

"I tell you," he roared, "we've got him this time, the hell-hound of the bulls! Our mitts are already on him, the dude, the dolled-up dick! I know that letter of mine will fetch him, little cockatoo! It takes a strutting bantam like that to throw a fury when he's sneered at and dared to anything. He'll run his two-by-two neck right into our noose all right, all right. We're going to get him this time, sure as hell!"

A rat-faced, pockmarked fellow of thirty or thereabouts jerked up a reptilian head flanked by bat ears. They had dubbed him Jack Ketch, not from the illustrious original, but because of his fiendish cleverness at strangulation. Jack Ketch, the second, had choked the life out of more than one victim. He bragged that he never used any other means for bumping off a quarry. Sometimes it was those hairy, stranglers hands of his, again a cord or some article from the helpless victim's clothing. This modern Jack Ketch was an ugly customer, albeit a valuable one to the Hyena and his gang. For he performed his killings swiftly, silently, without requiring special tools and without leaving ugly, identifying mementoes behind. So he had become the official executioner of the garroting gang.

The Hyena brought out his watch. It was a handsome jeweled

affair, choked out of Sellers, the oil king, when they had waylaid the magnate in his limousine not long ago. The police were still rabid at their inability to get the gangsters or to bring to book any one to pay the penalty for Sellers's killing.

"Nine thirty," announced the Hyena. "It's time to be off."

With sharp, incisive commands he ordered three of the gang to man the high-powered motor boat, idly rubbing its nose like some sea hound against the temporary landing place they had chosen for the evening's initial business. Three others, including Jack Ketch, entered a big black roadster parked outside the isolated boathouse.

With an ominous, ruthless roar the big car shot away in the darkness. Not so much as a gleam of light told of its remorseless progress.

CHAPTER III

THE ELEGANT FIGURE of Beau Quicksilver sat easily behind the wheel of the low-hung, racy roadster, that formidable Greyhound of justice which had leaped to the successful climax of many a hidden and weird mystery. With one hand lightly touching the wheel Quicksilver tore along over a dirt pike, soon to join the boulevard. The Greyhound's yellow orbs seared the darkness ahead like the eyes of some mythical monster.

Beau Quicksilver laughed to himself as though secretly pleased by some huge joke which kept amusing him. Once he had described a dark object peering out at him from the thick hedge surrounding one of the isolated estates. The Greyhound had merely disdainfully taken the bit in its teeth and torn away with redoubled speed. Then as the powerful roadster careened around a curve on three wheels a blaze of light flamed from the road dead ahead.

Figures like black imps tore about the leaping fire. For in the center of the road a car was burning merrily. Tongues of flame darted out from the engine along to the body of the machine. One man held up an arresting hand to Beau Quicksilver.

With the expert application of the brakes, the Greyhound came to a quick pause. Throwing open the door, the anomalous figure covered with a long, dark coat leaped out into the circle of light.

"She's a wreck all right," wailed one man. "Can't do a thing. A beauty, too—almost new."

Then things began to happen. As though by magic the flames in the planted car died out. They turned black under the swift application of a couple of extinguishers. Something was flung over Beau Quicksilver's head. The duped detective was conscious of a sickening, nauseating odor. Then he knew no more.

CHAPTER IV

ON A LONELY island far down the river, the gang jostled one another. They craned eager necks anxious to lose no whit of the rare sport soon to unfold before them. For once the hardened criminals showed real excitement. They watched expectantly a certain pine tree which stood out stark and bleak on the rock promontory, backed by evergreens. Atop this spot a single object held every leering glance like a magnet. For a sturdy, right-angled branch from the bleak pine stretched a sinister arm seaward. Attached to this tree tentacle was a rope with a most businesslike noose at its end. One almost fancied that the years had rolled backward a few centuries—that soon this modern pirate gang might sing out lustily in the argot of earlier buccaneer melody:

> "Fifteen men on the dead man's chest,
> Yo-ho, yo-ho, yo-ho—"

But the modern gibbet had not been erected for the taking-off of any old sea wasp. The waiting noose had been strung up by Jack Ketch's eager and painstaking fingers. It was his little joke, his entertainment for the edification of the gang.

For no less a prize than the hated dude detective, Beau Quicksilver, had fallen into their clutches but a few hours before. The slick sleuth had walked into the drawn snare like a blind bird, all unaware of the net spread for it. It was a gala evening—for the Hyena and his gang of law-breaking cutthroats.

Yet there was a certain spirit of restlessness rampant among them, despite the Hyena's dominating presence and the expert, cool movements of Jack Ketch. More than one head occasionally jerked toward the sea as if expecting some sudden apparition there. Other heads cast doubtful glances at the solemn, lowering sky. The whole atmosphere of the place breathed of the untoward. It was as though the elements themselves were already hanging a sable pall around that lonely ledge where the famous Beau Quicksilver should soon make his final exit.

There was a stir from the unlighted motor boat parked under the overhanging ledge just below the tree with its stark, sinister arm and its expectant noose. Two of the gang had been left on guard in the powerful craft. They emerged now, literally armed to the teeth. Between them walked a slight, satin-clad form. The men stood on tiptoe, peering at the figure dimly limned by the lanterns which the two jailers carried. They pressed a step nearer the gibbet before them.

Quicksilver's face was white. His shoulders sagged disconsolately. Somewhere in the fray he had lost his plumed hat. For once his thick, dark hair was unkempt and disheveled. The dandified figure appeared a mere stripling between the stalwart, muscular men who were piloting him. They were taking no chances with this slippery, elusive catcher of cunning criminals.

The tramp, tramp, tramp of the guard's heavy shot feet crunched over the rocks to the solitary, waiting pine on the ledge. The Hyena snapped out hoarse commands, posting his men at cautious intervals. Yet what he could fear on that isolated island ten miles from the mainland was problematical. His act suggested that the gangsters gaged Beau Quicksilver for a sleuth of no mean prowess, despite his light stature and his one hundred and fifty-five pounds.

The leering Jack Ketch stood ready with the noose. The slight, scarlet figure of Quicksilver stepped forth. His satin doublet, its disheveled lines hidden by the uncertain light, gleamed exceedingly rich against the darkness. His ruff stood out immaculately white.

Then, to the surprise of the waiting, expectant gang, Beau Quicksilver made them a graceful, mocking bow. He held one slim white hand against the empty scabbard dangling at his left side. Still retaining this position he uttered a few words to Jack Ketch. Something in his speech caused that bloodthirsty scoundrel to stare at him in amazement. Then he turned to the Hyena standing a bit behind him.

For a moment the Hyena frowned blackly. Then he threw back his beefy neck and laughed with a bull-like roar. Peal upon peal came from his brutish throat. Jack Ketch's ugly features lapsed into a sneering smirk. But Beau Quicksilver stood quietly, his head forward. He was the picture of dejection and resignation.

Then the Hyena strode forward. Peremptorily he raised a hand. A portentous quiet ensued. He bellowed out:

"What do you think! The damned dude is blubbering! He's made a death-bed wish. Begs a favor from *us* that he's been hounding for weeks. Knows he's a goner all right. And he's crying baby, the white-livered skunk! *What do you suppose he wants?*"

"What did the dirty dick ask for?" yelled one of the gang. "It's worth giving it to him just to pipe the blubber on his mug! Beau Q. spilling salt gobs! Say, that's a sight next to his corpse!"

"What does he want?" shouted somebody else.

Again the Hyena flung back his thick neck and roared with ribald laughter.

"He begs to die like a gentleman—like a *gentleman*, do you hear? Wouldn't that make you throw a fit?"

Again the Hyena's uproarious mirth echoed about the place.

"What do you mean?" called out one of the gang. "Don't he

want to be strung up like a side of beef? Ain't Jack Ketch's noose good enough for him?"

"No," answered the Hyena, still shaking with laughter. "The strutting dandy is fussy, you know. He's squeamish about the idea of rough, common rope against his tender throat. He begs us with tears in his eyes that the noose be looped about the high collar of his velvet jacket, that it may not touch or soil his lily-white skin! Oh, ho, ho, ho!"

"Ha, ha, ha! Ho, ho, ho!" echoed the gang. "The damned dandy! The fussy son of a fop! Ha, ha, ha! Ho, ho, ho!"

"What do you say?" cut in their leader.

"Sure! Let him die with the halter outside his velvet coat if he wants! He'll rest easier in hell, maybe. Sure thing. The blubber is worth it!"

With a mocking flourish Beau Quicksilver bowed to them again. Then he daintily dusted his lips with a fine kerchief which still remained in his otherwise empty pockets. He turned to the waiting Jack Ketch.

Darker and darker grew the sky. Low rumblings of thunder, like the moans of many of the gang's victims, came muttering in from over the sea. Livid lines of lightning occasionally rent the darkness. In them the gibbet stood out, stark and shadowy like an ugly black arm poised against the somber sky. All was hurry now to have the business at hand completed before the impending storm broke.

Jack Ketch took the rope. Beau Quicksilver himself, to the unwilling admiration of the gang, placed the stout noose in position about his velvet collar. His slight hands looked very delicate and white against the rich velvet. Even Jack Ketch could discern no tremor as the dude detective nonchalantly set the death noose around his own velvet throat.

There was a momentous pause. The thunder grew louder. The waves sounded an equally dramatic prelude.

Then the scarlet body of Beau Quicksilver shot out at the

end of the stout rope. It jerked once, twice, spasmodically. Then it hung limp over the tossing waters.

The storm now broke in unleashed fury. The gang hastened around to a cave in the rocks which they frequently made their lair. The Hyena and his ruthless band of cutthroats were satisfied. At last that scourge of justice, Beau Quicksilver, had been done for! At last they had gained a respite from the scarlet figure swinging at the end of the rope.

Only Jack Ketch, a devotee to business, remained to see that life was entirely extinct before hastening after the gang. He settled down in the lee of a rock to protect himself against the great sheets of rain which now pelted the land. As a livid streak of lightning illumined the promontory, he say the bedraggled, limp object swaying there.

Then the official hangman of the gang hurried toward the sheltered cave. Vividly etched in his crime-soaked memory, he carried the picture of a sprawling, dangling, black shadow which had once been the dapper Beau Quicksilver.

CHAPTER V

SOME TIME LATER the moon came out, dissipating the heavy storm clouds. From within the cavern came the sound of ribald, drunken laughter. For the Hyena and his gang had stowed aboard the big motor boat a plentiful supply of firewater to round up the night's celebration. Jack Ketch alone remained partially sober. For this ruthless crook took his ugly profession seriously. Now, thoroughly dried and warmed with a generous libation, he hurried back to the gibbet he had deserted so precipitously when the storm broke. But several times before he climbed over the rocks to the death tree he puckered his brow. The moonlight now bathed their island rendezvous with a ghostly, uncanny effulgence.

Once Jack Ketch stopped and muttered to himself. Then he frowned darkly and dashed his hands vehemently against his eyes, cursing the fiery liquid he had drunk. Still muttering to himself, he reached the rocky promontory. The sinister, swaying pine reared its stark head against the moonlit sky. The stars winked sneeringly. The sea chuckled and murmured. No wonder the elements proclaimed their satisfaction!

For against the moonlit sky the great branch on the death pine stood forth unmistakably. The rope dangled there plainly. *But it was empty!*

Jack Ketch reeled and blinked at the ugly, sprawling thing. Swearing foul oaths he stumbled forward. He put out a shaking hand as though to confirm what his eyes saw but could not believe. Yes. There was no doubt of it. The rope still swung from the tree arm. *But it had been neatly severed near the end!*

"Hell!" snarled Jack Ketch. "I—I'm seeing things! C-course he's here! Only he ain't!"

With a wide-eyed, backward glance at the empty rope Jack Ketch tore toward the gang. He burst in on them like a fury.

"He's g-gone!" he blubbered shrilly. "The damned dude's beat it! He's given us the slip with a noose around his neck. The bulls are here somewhere. Must be. They cut him down. They'll get us—any minute—"

His extraordinary words partially sobered the Hyena and the gang. The big leader tore out of the hiding place. He scrambled over the rocks, swearing, sputtering, barking his shins in his haste. The rest tumbled after him.

But when they came to the solitary pine only an empty rope dangled sneeringly before their very gaze. The moon smiled down on them grimly—knowingly.

"Somebody's got him!" roared the Hyena. "They dogged us here to cut him down and then land on us. The boat! The boat! Hurry! Let's all pile into the boat!"

Like a flock of loathsome buzzards the Hyena and his men tumbled down the rocks to the spot where they had left the high-powered craft.

Suddenly they stood back aghast.

For the motor boat they had parked there was gone—had melted away in the moonlight!

Only a starlit sea rippled mockingly before them.

CHAPTER VI

BEFORE DAWN STREAKED in, a police boat, piloted by a rakish, black power boat, tore away from the mainland to an island dotting the water some ten miles out. Crouched over the wheel in the forward craft sat a figure still clad in blood-red satin. As the moonlight touched the face of the man dressed so strangely for a criminal chase, one caught one's breath. For the debonair figure of Beau Quicksilver in the flesh sat steering the plunging craft at full speed ahead. Not so many hours before the same figure had stood, bowing mockingly and fearfully voicing a final request. Not so many hours before Jack Ketch himself had seen with an accomplished eye this same scarlet figure shot into eternity from the business end of a stout and entirely dependable rope.

Chief Cartman and Perm Markham strained their binoculars ahead.

"I fancy," murmured the chief, "that I can already decry a sinister, single pine rearing its black shape on the promontory."

Quicksilver flung back his dark head and laughed. One slender hand went to his throat. About the velvet collar a length of stout, knotted rope still clung with treacherous insistence.

"Pull off my left shoe, Penn, old man," he suggested above the pounding of the motor. "Under the sole is a flat, very keen blade. Just cut off this pleasant little memento, will you? I want to preserve it."

Reaching down, Penn Markham pulled off one of the buckled shoes. He plucked up the extra sole and brought out a flat length of gleaming steel. With a quick movement of his sinewy fingers, he severed the rope.

Then for the first time Beau Quicksilver opened his velvet jacket beneath its high-ruffed collar.

"Lend a hand here, Penn," he requested; "the thing fits like my skin."

As Markham complied, the chief held aloft a flash lamp. Under its rays the skin on Quicksilver's throat appeared very smooth and singularly motionless, unwrinkled as it was from under his ears halfway to the clavicle. Quicksilver pointed indicating fingers to his throat.

"So," he told Penn Markham, "and so."

As his assistant obeyed his suggestions two pieces of curved, exceedingly thin steel came away in his hands. They bore the exact shape of Quicksilver's throat and were painted flesh-colored.

"Ah," commented the slender sleuth, vigorously rubbing his own throat, "that fellow at Damascus, whom I visited when last abroad, is an incomparable artizan. His fashioning of this steel neckpiece according to my orders has not only spared my life, but put a gang of ruthless cutthroats at last within our grasp. I knew that I was just the proper bait to spring the trap on that garroting gang."

Chief Cartman suppressed a shiver.

"Pretty narrow chances you took, Quicksilver," he remarked. "It is a clever stunt and all that. And the capturing of this gang will be a great feather in your cap. But don't play with fire like that again. You're worth too much to us."

Beau Quicksilver shrugged as he toned to the wheel.

"Oh, it wasn't so risky," he observed slowly. "My most unpleasant moment was when I played the cry-baby stuff in order that I might adjust the noose myself. Not much of a chance in the dim light that that rascal Ketch would have noticed anything with my collar pulled down. But I couldn't afford to slip up. Rather uncomfortable dangling in mid-air for a bit, even with a steel neckpiece. 'Twas easy enough to reach into my shoe and yank out the bit of steel, then cut myself free. You know the rat."

The chief nodded. He flashed in code, swift commands to

the police boat behind I him. For the island now loomed up a sinister, isolated blot of black in a somnolent, silver sea.

The Hyena and his gang put up a desperate fight. But the reappearance of that redoubtable, mercurial Beau Quicksilver *in the flesh* dampened their ardor. And they were no match for the minions of the law, who outnumbered them, were sober, and who fired from well-armed boats or safe ambush.

Jack Ketch had performed his last rope trick. And the Hyena would no longer thirst for Beau Quicksilver's blood. The mystery master had again turned the trick. Rapierlike justice had once more banished bestial strength and criminal cunning.

THE GREEN RAJAH

CRAGMORELAND WAS IN the grip of a diabolical epidemic. But the prevalent pest was not that of disease. It pertained to a series of most audacious gem thefts. Moreover, the purloinings were consummated on a scale seldom met with, either in this country or abroad.

In the midst of the epidemic Chief Cartman of the police department was hastily summoned one morning to a private conclave in the office of Waite Claverly—a financial and commercial power in the community.

"I suppose," sneered the chief, "that you think you can give the department some dope on how to solve these jewel riddles! Undoubtedly you believe that the answer to the vanished baubles is just meat and drink to the layman! Or have you asked me here to set up another infuriated howl—"

Waite Claverly shrugged his shoulders.

"You haven't hit it yet," he remarked quietly, proffering a box of cigars.

Waite Claverly was president of an influential insurance company, as well as a big personal loser by one of the thefts. Mrs. Claverly had missed her marvelous diamonds at a dance given in the famous ballroom of the Hotel Galland. The Claverlys had made loud, repeated and violent protestations concerning the kidnaped necklace. The C.I.D. had done its level best. Uselessly, however. The diamonds, worth a queen's ransom, had flown on obscure, swift, but entirely effective wings. This crime, like others, had occurred almost under the very noses of the police.

Then the noted diva, Mlle. Zerani, was minus her string of perfect pearls. The robbery occurred shamelessly, and with great embarrassment to those present, at an exclusive afternoon tea given by Lady Allenwhite in honor of the popular songbird. Hereupon the police put down their square-toed, inelegant boots firmly. They penned the guests willy-nilly in the house of Lady Allenwhite. They searched the shocked inmates. They used a fine-toothed comb over the house. Again without result.

Straightway each and every guest set up such a ferocious roar at the indignity, that the police even now get hot under the collar at the mere mention of the distressing affair. So one might continue with the narration of other jewel thefts occurring under seemingly insoluble circumstances.

Waite Claverly's interest in running down the miscreants was twofold. In addition to the loss of Mrs. Claverly's valuable necklace, his firm was daily being importuned to pay out huge indemnities. For the major part of the jewels carried heavy insurance.

"The company has met in executive session," confided Waite Claverly to Chief Cartman. "The gem thefts have got to stop. The papers and the people at large are still protesting violently even though your department is doing its best. There is only one man who can dig out the answer—"

Chief Cartman raised his big head. "You're right. To hell with the Seine drownings and the needs of the Prefect of Police at Paris! We've got to have Beau Quicksilver back in a hurry!"

"Now you're talking!" agreed Waite Claverly. "Here's a cable form."

Puffing like a volcano, Chief Cartman grabbed the sheet. He wrote in barbed code. The S.O.S. summons set down with a reckless disregard of expense a skeleton outline of the amazing jewel robberies. And he finished the mandate with those very agreeable words, "Expense no object."

The cablegram was dispatched with all possible celerity. In due time:

"Coming on the Xavia," flashed back Beau Quicksilver.

CHAPTER II

A GOODLY CROWD assembled for the docking of the Xavia. The big ocean liner had dropped anchor in the harbor the night before. For she had steamed in after hours, and her passengers could not be landed until the quarantine guardians of public safety boarded her the next morning. While the passengers fumed and fretted, the big wireless sputtered and chuckled with fiery glee. Messages in code went skipping skyward, ultimately to be transferred from their celestial orbit to decidedly mundane destinations.

At last the gangplank was down. The big sea-monster began to disgorge its cargo of human freight. Norling, a reporter from the *Breeze,* occupied a front place by the restraining rope. An admiring companion was with him.

"Got wind that there's a notable bunch aboard," he confided, slipping a couple of extra plates into his celebrity shooter as he poised the camera in readiness.

Then the first passenger alighted—a dapper, fashionably attired figure in the nobbiest of great-coats and swinging a Mahowa cane.

"Did you pipe that guy there?" whispered Norling. "That's Beau Quicksilver, the famous dude detective, answering a hurry call from headquarters. Got to get the answer to these whole-sale gem kidnapings. They'd loaned him to the Parisian police. But I understand they cabled him to beat it in a hurry. Say, he's the Marconi of the criminal world. A regular wiz. Clever! Why, nobody can even guess what the fellow does know! Regular mine of queer information."

The smartly clad newcomer flipped back his coat to an official. On seeing the little silver badge there, that custom's dignitary passed his luggage without even the formality of a search.

Then the slight, swagger figure peremptorily put up a suede-gloved finger for a taxi. In a twinkling the door shut him from sight and the cab shot away.

At this moment there was a stir and the craning of necks. A grande dame was disembarking accompanied by her suite. The woman's haughty bearing and snow-white hair would set her apart anywhere. It branded her as a somebody without the necessity for any formal introduction.

"Some valuable birds aboard," continued Norling. "That's the Countess Zer and her retainers. She's here for a social season. They say her jewels would make a queen choke with envy. Among them is the Green Rajah. It is said to be a magnificent, pear-shaped emerald. Nobody knows its value in money. The countess comes at a critical time. For if I were a crook I should throw an itching at the palms to nab that big, sea-green bauble."

Two of the titled stranger's party parleyed with the customs inspector and remained with the stack of luggage bearing the Zer coat-of-arms. Meantime the countess and her remaining attendants entered two huge limousines and disappeared from the sight of the gaping crowd.

CHAPTER III

WITH THE COMING of the aristocratic lady from overseas, Cragmoreland's wholesale jewel crimes were temporarily forgotten. And no wonder! For the noble visitor distinguished herself almost immediately as a person of dazzling brilliancy, and of clever bon mots. Her repartee was at times almost epigrammatic. Cragmoreland sat up and took notice.

The Countess Zer and her notable retinue were soon established in the town-house of the Claverlys—a lease of the fine mansion becoming possible with the departure of the Claverlys for an ocean voyage on their yacht. The Countess Zer immediately entered upon a round of social affairs. She was feted and entertained lavishly. Her wardrobe was the envy and despair of all feminine Cragmoreland. Assuredly the elegant, snowy-haired dame believe that variety was the spice—nay the very essence—of daily apparel.

But added to her beautiful wardrobe were her gems. These were the last straw to break the backs of any hesitating stiff-necks. Her collection was marvelous. She seemed to have gems to match each gown. Daily Cragmoreland watched and wondered. They were avid for a glimpse of the wonderful Green Rajah—said to be the world's finest emerald. Yet with tantalizing remissness, the Countess Zer did not appear with the pear-shaped gem strung about her throat on its platinum chain. Cragmoreland felt cheated. They hungered for a glimpse of the stone.

Then, one momentous day, the Countess Zer's imposing limousine with the Zer coat-of-arms emblazoned on the door, drove up with a flourish of cylinders and a fanfare of adulatory glances to the offices of the chief of police. The lady made a considerable visit within that drab interior.

Subsequently it was whispered in the papers, like a stage aside, that the Countess Zer had sought police protection for her wonderful gems after hearing considerable alarming conversation concerning the hauls which had recently been taking place.

This knowing whisper soon gained substance. For almost immediately afterward the Countess Zer sent out invitations for a week-end which was to wind up with her first ball. Yet, in all, only two dozen invitations went forth to cause havoc and hatred among certain aspiring hearts in Cragmoreland. The buzzing increased daily. Assuredly the Countess Zer ignored precedent with a lavish and autocratic hand. But the chosen few plumed and prepared themselves for the momentous occasion.

Already it was noised about that at this ball the Countess Zer would wear for the first time the famous Green Rajah. Subtlely queried on the matter, the Countess Zer smiled knowingly and discussed the Russian ballet. Then Cragmoreland knew for a certainty that the Green Rajah would be worn for the first time on the night of the ball.

Big limousines, snappy roadsters and every other genus of the automobile family, rolled up the splendid drive to the Countess Zer's Cragmoreland "castle." The weekend was on with a flourish. Cragmoreland held its breath—and waited expectantly for the ball. The entire atmosphere of the city was strung up for some unexpected denouement. And now that the first glamour surrounding the titled lady had dimmed a bit, the sinister circumstances surrounding the momentarily forgotten gem hauls returned with redoubled vigor.

The time preceding the ball passed all too swiftly for the super-elect who numbered the Countess Zer's chosen few. Since the reporters received no new copy concerning what was going on within, they contented themselves with a rehash of certain bon mots of the distinguished lady.

"A person's *arteries* don't harden—it's his *ideas*," the countess had responded to the would-be personal gibe made by Mrs. Porter-Rockford when she solicitously inquired if the visiting stranger had yet been troubled with that malady. Again, she was asked by the young social favorite, Lalla Marlborough, a stately beauty, "Now, Countess Zer, do tell us what Continental artists consider the ideal height for a woman." Promptly Countess Zer answered, "Five feet four and three-quarters." "But I am five feet seven," pouted Lalla Marlborough. "Ah," flashed back the countess, "you, my dear young lady, are more than ideal!"

Within the temporary abode of the Countess Zer full-fledged preparations continued for the ball.

But the brilliant social function was doomed not to occur. For at eight twenty-five on that unforgettable evening the Countess Zer dashed out of her suite. Her hair was disheveled, her beautiful dressing-robe twisted and awry.

"My ancestral heritage!" she screamed two tones higher than her usual high-pitched voice. "The Green Rajah! It's gone!"

Then two unknown guests stepped forward. They were plain-clothes men, loaned by the police for any emergency. They moved with belated but sincere rapidity. They called up the chief. Presumably that dignitary swore vehemently in unprintable billingsgate. He dispatched a motorcycle corps to the house immediately.

The facts were few. The Countess Zer had merely stepped from her sleeping-chamber into her dressing-room for the briefest time—not more than three minutes, she declared. She had just brought forth the Green Rajah from its secret hiding-place—which to this day remains unknown. She had placed it on her dressing-table, which stood between the two windows across the room from the dressing-room door. And when she went back the Green Rajah was gone.

The guests were instantly detained in the house. Men were posted at all exits. There was no possibility of a single premature escape.

Bellamy, a young man from headquarters, took charge of the preliminary skirmishings. He issued orders like a martinet.

"Now you first, Madame la Comtesse," he suggested briskly.

He was using as his temporary inquisitorial chamber the big sitting-room on the second floor which he had commandeered for the unpleasant task. The guests he had ordered to remain in their rooms where they presumably had been when the Green Rajah vanished.

"Was the door of your sleeping-room locked, madame?" he asked.

The countess, pale and distrait, twisted her satin dressing-gown. "But no, *monsieur*. I thought I had shot the bolt. Alas, now it appears that this was not so. I should not otherwise have left the Green Rajah for a second had I believed the room to be unlocked."

Young Bellamy jotted down the fact in an imposing looking notebook.

"I'll look into that," he said. "It bears examination. If you did shoot the bolt—uselessly—well, we shall see. Now, have I the layout of your suite correctly? Your sleeping-chamber from whose dresser the Green Rajah was taken, is the middle room between your sitting-room and your dressing-room. There are connecting doors between these rooms and each one has a door on the corridor?"

"Of a verity, that is so."

"Now, beyond your dressing-room into which you stepped for the briefest time is only your bathroom with its single entrance into the dressing-room?"

She nodded affirmation.

"Were the corridor doors of the other rooms locked when you discovered the robbery?"

"Yes, they were, and still remain so."

Bellamy tapped on his notebook with his pencil. "Your servants now, are they trustworthy?"

"They all come splendidly recommended. But that isn't all," she added with agitation.

"Well?" he asked bluntly.

"That Mr. Green, whom your chief sent down from headquarters, was posted in the alcove at the foot of the stairs to see that no one came up. And the other man—I do not recall his name—was in the vicinity of the other staircase—"

"Which entirely eliminates the servants," granted Bellamy. "Awkward, isn't it?"

"Mon Dieu! C'est terrible—terrible—"

"May I see the list of your invited guests?"

"I have it with me. I had anticipated that request." With trembling fingers she proffered him a sheet of paper.

For a moment, only the rustle of the list and Bellamy's narrowed lids told of anything unusual occurring within the guarded house.

Then he whistled. "Pretty kettle of fish! Every name here is a regular bulwark of respectability—a monument of family, money and breeding!"

The countess raised her aristocratic brows a bit haughtily. "The list was the result of much cogitation. I would invite only the elite of your city. The proletariat and the *nouveau riches* are so crass. They irk me like cubist painting, free verse and stucco. They are so very new and garish, don't you know?"

"Ya—as," answered Bellamy glibly. Then he reddened to the tips of his ears. But she seemed unconscious of his impertinent retort.

"Well, there is nothing to it," he decided, "but to make a personal examination of each guest. I'll phone headquarters for a matron. Before I begin the personal inspection I'll give the billiard room on this floor the once-over to be sure the gem isn't cached there. Then as fast as we go through each guest we'll corral him—or her—in this previously searched billiard room. If a personal examination does not produce the Green Rajah, I shall go through each guest's room, not once but several times. *For the gem must be in this house, either on the person of the thief or cunningly salted somewhere.*"

"A tremendous task," sighed the lady.

"Yes, but not impossible of result. Heretofore, in this epidemic of jewel robberies, the cases have been bungled at the outset. There have been loopholes. This time there are none. The gem is hermetically sealed in this house, as it were."

The countess arose to depart. She had aged unbelievably. The wrinkles showed now with the makeup forgotten.

"You know," she said significantly, before opening the door, "that a great reward is the price for quick and expert investigation. The gem *must be recovered.*"

"I'll do my best, madam," he answered. Then the countess retired hastily to her own apartments.

CHAPTER IV

BELLAMY SEARCHED THE billiard room. He was satisfied that there was nothing there. Then, one by one, the indignant and protesting guests were marshaled for the personal search. Each one who entered could show as an alibi a pedigree the proverbial foot long, an impressive bankroll, and near-scandal-proof social connections. As the countess had said, she had skimmed only the rich cream from Cragmoreland's exclusive social set.

While Bellamy and the matron in turn were overtly busy with each person in the sitting room, another figure crept with noiseless and lightning rapidity from room to room of each guest. The sixth member of the exclusive assemblage had hardly disappeared into the billiard room, when this slight, stealing figure hurried down to a phone in a sound-proof box at the foot of the stairs.

A low colloquy ensued. "Chief. All right. *You know my voice.* Chief, get to Lalla Marlborough's residence at once. Find out for me if—" Then the mysterious, elusive figure spoke directly into the mouthpiece.

Fifteen minutes later this same stealthy figure slid up the stairs, three steps at a time. He knocked on the door of the commandeered room.

"Bellamy," he ordered crisply, "go to the billiard room. Ask Miss Marlborough to come here at once."

"B-but, sir, the matron has already examined her," answered young Bellamy perplexedly. "She just left."

"Bring her back," insisted the slim stranger, and he strode to a window.

Shortly an exceedingly furious and stunning looking woman re-entered.

"What does this repeated outrage mean?" she demanded. "You shall smart for this! I'll have my attorneys—"

Like a slight-of-hand performer the unknown stranger made a quick, expert movement. A woman's enraged and baffled scream followed.

For in his hand lay the well-known bronze mode of coiffure characteristic of Lalla Marlborough. A woman of blondish hair faced him. Moreover, with the removal of the wig, so carefully fashioned and tinted to resemble startlingly Lalla Marlborough's hair, a subtle change had crept into the woman's features. Fury had wrought some of the metamorphosis. She looked less like the oft-pictured, well-known social favorite.

"Gee!" exclaimed young Bellamy, "as I'm a dick—*it's a double!* A dead ringer for Miss Marlborough with the wig on, and minus the fury! Can you beat it?"

"You'll find," went on the slim unknown, "with the application of grease and other makeup removers, that the lady," he bowed mockingly, "will not so closely resemble the absent Lalla Marlborough. I have just learned from the chief that Miss Marlborough was strangely missing from her home for dinner when she should have been there making final preparations for the affair here. The answer becomes clear. Miss Marlborough was kidnaped, held an unwilling captive, that this woman might play her part and take possession of her wardrobe."

"Can you beat it! Where is the real lady?"

"We shall soon see," answered the inquisitor firmly.

Then, as the others left the room, he began his questioning of the unmasked woman before him.

CHAPTER V

"IT'S AN EXTRAORDINARY development in crime," averred Beau Quicksilver, who, as you may have guessed, was the mysterious stranger who had appeared so very opportunely at the countess's abode to unmask the clever impersonator of Lalla Marlborough. "The woman in the case is known to this superior, new, criminal clique as The Chameleon for her really extraordinary ability to reflect personality in manner and voice as well as facial expression. To be sure, there are other women in the gang who play dual roles as well. But this one was chosen because of her rather close resemblance to Miss Marlborough, for her mental alertness and her daring. These new crooks are headed by a new type of Fagin. The man has trained a bunch, women principally, to play high-class Raffles roles for the purpose of spiriting away rare jewels. They work in many ways, most often as servants. Then they bribe the kidnaped maid or valet with money enough to keep dark the enforced absence—while the masquerading crook plays the role and takes the gems. As you know, we have not only rounded up the ring of jewel-thieves and impersonators, but we have learned the truth concerning the clever crimes."

Penn Markham smiled. "A big job," he said, "—a rich haul!"

Quicksilver continued, "We dragged the truth out of Lalla Marlborough's impersonator first. Made her tell where her real double was held. The rest was easy. While Bellamy or the matron searched each guest, I gave that particular person's room a thoroughgoing examination. When the pseudo Miss Marlborough was in the billiard room, I located the stolen and hidden Green Rajah."

"I am curious as to where she concealed it," confessed Penn Markham.

"You couldn't guess in an elephant's age," smiled Beau Quicksilver. "Only the smell of linseed oil put me on the trail. My olfactory nerves are trained, you know."

Penn Markham smiled reminiscently. "I have reason to know," he recalled.

"The fake Miss Marlborough with rooms opposite the Countess Zer's—" Quicksilver smiled whimsically—"had previously doctored the bolt in the countess's sleeping-room door, so that it would stop just short of locking. When this bolt was presumably shot, you see, nothing happened to make the room entrance-proof."

"Clever," nodded Markham, "but ordinary."

"The rest is not. The lady took long chances in opening that door. But had the Countess Zer discovered her she would undoubtedly have coolly asked for smelling-salts or a lip-stick— and tried again. But everything was bound to go well for her. It was the work of a moment to open the bedroom door, slip across the rich carpet to the dresser, and help herself to the gem. She was out again and behind her own locked door before the theft was discovered. She had a hiding-place all prepared. This is where my nose put me wise. For as I went over the room, even tapping the dark woodwork for some hidden panel, I caught the smell of linseed oil high in the wood on the door frame. The reason was soon patent. The Chameleon had bored a hole with an inch auger-bit into the flat, plain, dark wood of the door-casing. She made the hiding-spot high up, probably standing on a chair, and she is tall. This height would strengthen the illusion that the woodwork remained natural and intact. For when she slipped the Green Rajah into the prepared hole she merely temporarily covered the gem with a wad of plastine the exact shade of the wood. This she leveled off flat with the surface of the plain door-casing. It would stand the closest scrutiny. Plastine, you know, is the new form of modeling wax used by sculptors in preference to clay because the oil in its composition keeps it pliable. It comes in many shades. I smelled the linseed oil. But no painting had been done in the room.

Then I kept prodding around the area of the smell with my fingers. So I found the soft spot."

"Were all the jewels that have been taken cached in such a way?"

"Along the same lines. Other spots in the woodwork or under the furniture were bored into, and different shades of plastine were used to match the wood."

"Hm-m," observed Penn Markham, "quite an idea!"

"Well," went on Beau Quicksilver, "it has cost the irate losers of the gems, and Waite Claverly's company, a pretty penny to stage this big showdown. But they are satisfied. Much of the loot has been recovered. The lawbreakers have been brought to book. So a pretty crafty bunch of crooks won't trouble the community for some years to come. Besides, baiting the trap was rare sport."

"You were superb," admired Penn Markham. "Quite unbelievable!"

"It was a magnificent, faked emerald—a synthetic stone that would have fooled an expert as it did The Chameleon."

"Ah," commented Markham, "but the gem wasn't half as much of a sell as was—"

"Extra! Extra! All about the fake Countess Zer! All about the dude detective's impersonation of an unknown noblewoman! Extra! Extra!" came the shrill cry of the newsboys.

"The city won't get over laughing for many weeks to come," roared Penn Markham. "The titled stranger will go down as history in criminal annals. As that paradoxical enigma, the Countess Zer, you were incomparable. The stage lost a great actor when you elected to become a great crime chaser!"

"I should worry," retorted Beau Quicksilver with a shrug. "For that matter, you yourself displayed real histrionic ability in playing my double. You were rich from the start. I can still see you, strutting down the gangplank and imperiously waving up a cab in true Quicksilver style. Classy acting, Penn, old man. Let's make it a pair!"

BLISTERING TONGUES

WHEN BEAU QUICKSILVER, known as that "damned dude dick" to all crookdom, arrived at the scene of the mystery, the belching chimney smoke had long since feathered out to nothingness. The Amesbury homestead was indeed peculiarly well situated for any dark deed. It was set in a clump of pines which poked dark, melancholy prongs against the clotting dusk of eventide. And rank vegetation ran riot beyond the trees. For Mark Amesbury had been an erratic, odd stick, who cared not a tinker's dam for public opinion or the uncomplimentary epithets that spattered like hail about him.

The huge bulk of Chief Cartman of the C.I.D. heaved itself cumbersomely to its feet at Quicksilver's ring.

As the sleek, immaculately clad back of the dandified figure was gulped into the grim interior of the silent house, a chauffeur in the Amesbury garage turned an excited, adulatory glance toward a mechanic.

"Golly, Dick—that's the guy all right! That's the fellow, Beau Quicksilver—regular 1923 model, racy lines, twelve cylinders, aluminum engine! And believe me, old stick-in-the-grease, he's the master mechan' when there's a hurry call from police head-quarters for a real trouble shooter. Hits on all twelve cylinders all the time. Not a miss. And speedy! Well, say, he's the Tommy Milton on the crime raceway here. Regular self-starter, he is! And as fussy for decent fuel as the niftiest carburetor that ever pushed a buzz-wagon. Something doing here, O.K. When old Amesbury passes in his checks, there's sure to be hell to pay."

While this panegyric was being mouthed in the garage, Beau Quicksilver lounged in a chair in a compact, denlike room flanking the entrance to the sprawling Amesbury domicile. Chief Cartman squatted excitedly on a leather upholstered chair which shrank to pygmy lines under his elephantine bulk.

The famous crime chaser in the smartest of gray, from fedora to spats, lolled nonchalantly, idly twirling a heavily chased ring on the little finger of his left hand. To the casual observer he appeared eaten up with ennui as he awaited Cartman's explanation for the hurry call that had brought him to the somber house of the eccentric Mark Amesbury.

Cartman cupped a knee with a squat, spatulate hand. He leaned far forward. He spoke with staccato brusqueness—a characteristic he always displayed when mentally excited, and when the onus of much responsibility fell suddenly on his Atlaslike shoulders. For Cartman held a superlative respect for the mighty dollar; and Mark Amesbury possessed very great wealth.

"Chinese puzzle, all right, Quicksilver," the chief spat out vehemently, giving his knee a resounding thwack.

Beau Quicksilver crossed a slim, elegantly creased leg. His deep-set gray eyes seemed oblivious of the eager, pudgy face watching him with doglike fidelity.

"Well?" he drawled, for there had been cases where Cartman's preliminary enthusiasm had petered out to some common crime. "Well? Swing in the facts from the start. Cut the frills."

Cartman shrugged his shoulders. But confidence that a real mystery awaited the master hand of the finical Quicksilver still lighted his features. Full well he knew that bludgeoning butchery or ordinary mystery spelled anathema to the fastidious super-sleuth facing him.

Cartman cleared his throat and pulled his words together. "Got a call half an hour ago from here. Caretaker on the line.

Soared voice full of horror. Stated that Amesbury was locked in the Egyptian Room. Refused to hear repeated calls for supper. Dead silence within. Only two windows in the room. High, cell-like affairs, barred and bolted. The Egyptian Room carries a collection worth a king's ransom. So the defunct Amesbury took no chances. The servant was afraid to break in. So I beat it in the roadster along with Olmstead, who's guarding the room now. The door refused our shoulder third degree; so I shot my way in. And, gad, Quicksilver, 'twas some dope dream I stumbled into."

Beau Quicksilver's tempered steel glance gouged the chief's countenance. The mystery sleuth sat as immobile as a Ming mandarin. He might have been carved from joss. Not unmindful of Quicksilver's flattering attention, the chief ran on.

"Queerest hole I ever stumbled into, that room. It's like a chamber out of a museum. Cluttered up with heathen stuff, moth-eaten and old enough to grow whiskers. Idols, statues, mummies— Well, you'll see. And Amesbury, Quicksilver— where in hell do you suppose we found the guy?"

Still, Quicksilver sat motionless, his basilisk glance boring the chief's face.

Cartman shot a fist into his hand. "As you're a dick, Quicksilver, Mark Amesbury lay deader than a doornail, flat on his back in an Egyptian mummy case that was as old as Methuselah before Noah launched the ark."

For another second Quicksilver regarded him. Then like the ping of a .45: "Any mark of violence—any sign of foul play?"

"That's the hell of it. Body's smooth as a smelt. Nothing wrong with it, even through a microscope."

"What about the eyes?" shot out Quicksilver.

"Closed," retorted Cartman. "But examination of the pupils shows neither enlargement nor contraction. Not a hazy hint of any kind of poisoning."

Quicksilver smiled suddenly, boyishly. The expression transformed his usually ascetic features into a look of intense eagerness and benignity. He was like a boy who suddenly glimpses a coveted hour's swim in the old pool—with the woodpile some hours off.

The slim sleuth brought out a monogrammed silver cigarette case. Deftly he selected a tiny imported roll and lighted it.

"Ah, Cartman," he approved. "Smells good. Trot out some more."

"I thought you'd warm up a bit when you knew the details," observed Cartman. "There wasn't a thing amiss in the room that I could see. No sign of a struggle; not a finger print; not a suspicious mark or clue. Moreover, Amesbury was hermetically sealed in the room, so to speak."

"Any expression of fear or pain on the features?" inquired Quicksilver.

"Not a line. He might have been asleep."

"What about the skin?"

"Nothing."

"You spoke of two barred windows, high in the wall. Were they open?"

"Yes, both of them."

"Was the mummy case with Amesbury's body under the open windows?"

"No. On the south side at right angles to the windows."

"Did you give the ground outside the windows the once-over?"

Cartman sniffed disgustedly.

"Say, while I'm no Beau Quicksilver, I'm not quite a green-goods man in crime. Sure thing, I went over the ground. Nothing there. Not the sign of a footprint. The grass is freshly seeded. So it would show up the slightest suspicious thing. If you're trying to hint that some crafty Borgia stood outside and shot in some lethal lemon from a liquid gun or some other newfangled, diabolical gas shooter—spear the idea. Nothing to it. That was my first thought."

Quicksilver shrugged his gray shoulders disdainfully. "Bah, Cartman! You have missed a sign on the wall that's as big as a barn door. I've heard enough. Let's see this mysterious Egyptian Room and what it contains."

Almost joyously Quicksilver snuffed his cigarette and darted from the room with Cartman stepping smartly in his wake.

CHAPTER II

THE CHIEF HAD spoken without flamboyance. The death chamber was a bizarre place—significantly suited for any black mystery carrying labyrinthian details. It needed but a glance as he stood inside to tell Quicksilver that a vast sum of money was represented in that grim, silent and stealthy interior, whose collector now lay a stark, cold thing gripped to the heart of one of the most priceless curios—the mummy case which had once jealously hoarded the shriveled, brown body of an Egyptian king.

The chamber was large, even for an ordinary residence—high-posted and paneled throughout in rich, time-stained walnut. With the exception of the aforementioned dungeonlike windows high in the wall opposite the door which offered the only ingress, the room was lighted by a powerful overhead electrolier. In fact, the gloomy, Stygian atmosphere of the room must have made artificial illumination necessary most of the time when the owner of Amesbury House delved among the dust of the ages.

Quicksilver's lightning glance played about the room with its hodge-podge of relics. He saw a magnificent squat statue of Vishnu dominating the center with its slant eyes staring balefully, almost malevolently, upon the intruders. From object to object Quicksilver's steely gaze coursed. He was like some superbloodhound, nostrils aquiver for the first scent of the truth.

Then his eyes went directly to the grisly, long, brown shape which, like an ugly, venomous cocoon enwrapped Mark Amesbury in the last embrace of death.

The mummy case was a magnificent example from the reign of Theti I. The dusk of the ages was heavy upon it, toning down the garishness of yellow ocher and red clay. Yet, as Quicksilver walked slowly toward the brown sarcophagus there was nothing sinister or mysterious in the outlines of the thing. He had seen countless others, none finer perhaps, but all fashioned along similar lines.

Reluctantly, yet eagerly, Quicksilver's eyes abandoned their acute examination of the mummy case. His glance fell on the white, still face of Mark Amesbury already gripped in the winding sheet of old Egypt without the services of a modern mortuarian.

Cartman had spoken with exactitude. The face appeared placid, untouched by any signs either of external or internal violence.

Quicksilver swung about. "You said you examined the body. Since the mummy case sheaths it up to the armpits, you had it out?"

Cartman nodded affirmation.

Quicksilver frowned. "You know," he stated succinctly, "that you shouldn't have done that. It may have spoiled a dozen indicative signs. Maybe you have bungled the most vital clue. I have half a mind—"

But as Quicksilver's petulant glance swung about the room he shrugged his shoulders. With the motion his quick choler at the possible destruction of vital evidence was whisked into thin air.

"Lend a hand here," he said, almost good-naturedly. "But, by Jove—"

Quicksilver stood riveted. His eyes glowed as though illuminated by some sudden, blinding light from within. His flashing glance was no longer on the mummy case with its gruesome contents. His enlightened look seemed to be directed toward the wall immediately behind the death case.

Cartman followed Quicksilver's blazing scrutiny. "If you think that that paneled wall has any secret contraptions, you're barking up a wrong tree," he remarked. "There is not a hollow panel in the room."

"Blistering tongues of Hades!" Quicksilver murmured *sotto voce*. But to Cartman he said aloud: "The paneling doesn't interest me; but the radiator does."

With a quick, terse gesture he indicated the gilded outlines of the steam pipes which glimmered out richly against the dark paneling directly behind the mummy case.

With a ludicrous effort Cartman studied the radiator. For long association with Beau Quicksilver told him that here was a vital symbol, the first thread in the snarled skein of the puzzle.

With a bovine, incredulous expression Cartman's triple glances alternately included the dynamic sleuth, the dead face of Mark Amesbury, and the incriminating steam pipes.

"I pass," he murmured. "I don't get you, if you mean— Nope. It's Greek to me. What's the answer?"

Quicksilver raised his shoulders. "It's only a glimmer at present. I need further facts. But it has given me a whale of an idea. And if I can corroborate it—well, Cartman, it will be a *rara avis* that we've netted—a real, honest-to-goodness, black crime. Glory to Allah! Mayhap all the criminals haven't turned politicians yet. Now, let me get this household doped out right. You've mentioned the caretaker who sent in the alarm. What other members have we?"

Cartman considered. "That's the dickens of it. Amesbury lived the life of a recluse, an anchorite. He has a caretaker and a serving man. There is nobody else."

"Are there no relatives?"

Cartman shrugged his ponderous shoulders. "I have a hazy idea there is a brother—a nut on fungi—a professor in some small Limburger university. But the idea will have to be verified. Motive is decidedly clouded at present. Where do we go from here, Quicksilver?"

"I want a few moments in this room by myself," rejoined the detective. "I desire to verify, or try to prop up that blistering radiator notion of mine. And you, by the way, while I am closeted here, ask Olmstead to interrogate the caretaker. I wish to know if there was a fire in the furnace this afternoon. I am practically positive that there was, because the radiator has been recently gilded and I can still faintly detect the odor of banana oil commingled with heat."

"A fire in the furnace!" ejaculated Cartman. "And on a summer afternoon! What an idea, Quicksilver! Listens leary. Unless Amesbury was a victim of rheumatism and required much heat. He was a thin, bloodless-looking beggar, and looked as though he might run to rheumatics."

"I see no indications of rheumatism," retorted Quicksilver curtly. "But get that dope on the furnace fire. I'll be through here in a few moments."

Then the huge, dark-stained door shut Quicksilver's further investigations from the chief's disappointed gaze.

CHAPTER III

THIRTY MINUTES LATER Olmstead, the man from
headquarters, knocked diffidently on the dusky door of the
silent mystery room. There was a funereal pause. Just as the
bluecoat raised gnarled, knuckled fingers for a more vehement
summons, the door yawned.

Beau Quicksilver stood on the threshold. His gray eyes
glowed with flashing fires—the light of successful inquiry into
an obtuse crime. Olmstead knew the expression. It portended
well for the criminal investigation already swinging into momentum.

"Come in, Olmstead," invited Quicksilver affably.

He indicated an odd, mildewed stone bench in a corner
facing the sinister sarcophagus in which lay the lifeless body of
the Egyptologist.

"There *was* a fire," asserted Quicksilver. Yet there was no
interrogation in his voice. He spoke as one having authority.

"You've said it," retorted Olmstead. "Both the caretaker and
old Hepplewhite have verified the fact. There was a terrific fire
in the furnace this afternoon."

"Who ordered that fire?" shot out Quicksilver.

"Amesbury himself."

"Why?" demanded the sleuth. "What reason did the erratic
Egyptologist give for a consuming heat on a hot summer afternoon?"

"Old Hepplewhite declares," answered Olmstead blankly,
"that Amesbury wanted the heat as a drier. He said he had been
doing a bit of painting in the Egyptian Room and wanted to
speed up the drying of it."

Quicksilver's eyes flashed. "Excellent. Perfect corroboration."

Olmstead's eyes, however, continued to encircle the dark and
mysterious interior. The headquarters man even got up and

examined the room, aided by the powerful electrolier. Finally he paused before Quicksilver.

"Do you know," he began falteringly, "I've got a hound of a nose. But I can't get a whiff of fresh turpentine or linseed in these diggings. And I don't see a sign of fresh paint. These paneled walls are walnut, highly waxed and unstained by pigment. *What* did Mark Amesbury paint, Quicksilver? The thing grows blacker every minute."

"Ah," smiled Quicksilver. "That's because you are trying to light the wrong tunnel in this underground riddle. Blistering tongues of hell," he repeated.

Still Olmstead gazed at him as though he spoke in the heathen jargon of ancient Egypt, whose relics surrounded them and whose temple of death wrapped Mark Amesbury in an inescapable winding-sheet.

Alertly Quicksilver strode to the door, a cigarette clamped between his teeth.

"I'm off, Olmstead. All we need now is the culprit. The case approaches its climax."

And leaving a highly curious and deeply puzzled policeman on guard before the death-chamber door, Beau Quicksilver rejoined the chief who was interrogating Hepplewhite in the little den near the entrance door.

"Ah, Hepplewhite," greeted Quicksilver. "I want a word with you, with your permission, Cartman."

"Fire away," agreed the chief, mopping a beady brow and settling back in the chair with an air of baffled resignation.

"Who was your master's intimate confrere—associate in the study of Egyptian relics?" inquired Quicksilver.

"Professor Malotti," instantly responded Hepplewhite.

"Ah," commented Quicksilver softly, almost purringly, "the assistant curator at the museum here. I know the name well— its owner indifferently by reputation."

"A great scholar and a learned gentleman," answered Hepplewhite with awestruck accents.

"When was Professor Malotti here last, Hepplewhite?"

The old man pondered conscientiously. "He was here yesterday morning, sir."

"Ah," exclaimed Quicksilver. "Very good. Was he closeted with your master in the Egyptian room?"

"Yes, sir. They always kept their investigations to that room."

"Where does Professor Malotti live?"

"Number 12, Upton Terrace."

"Very good. Cartman, step on the gas. It's No. 12, Upton Terrace, in a hurry. The erudite scarab chaser and palimpsest hunter is now deep in the throes of museum duties. The time is ripe for a quick glance over his lodgings. Then we shall see how the land of the Borgias and Machiavelli has joined hands with the Kingdom of the Ptolemies and the Sphinx."

Cartman's face was sponged of any enlightening expression. "Malotti," he protested. "Why, the professor is a great authority and a scholar—the discoverer of much valuable data concerning ancient Egyptian civilization. What has he to do with it?"

Quicksilver held up an arresting hand.

"Not yet, but soon," he answered joyfully. "Let's go."

And old Hepplewhite, concealed behind the heavy damask curtains, watched with puzzled, frowning eyes the big roadster eat up the distance on the broad highway to the startling truth.

CHAPTER IV

A PRECISE AND dignified landlady protested against the sacrilege of police investigation in the sacred precincts of the Egyptian authority.

"It's all very strange," she murmured. "Is there anything wrong? Professor Malotti is a most courteous gentleman and very prompt in paying for his rooms."

Considerately Beau Quicksilver silenced her perturbation.

With a skeleton key the two investigators soon stood within the coveted interior.

Professor Malotti did himself well, very well. He occupied three large rooms and bath at the rear of the second floor. The largest of the three chambers was a combination workshop and curio container. The room was high posted and displayed many rare relics from ancient Egypt.

Beau Quicksilver stepped instantly to a big safe hidden by a curtain in a corner behind a miniature replica of the Sphinx. The detective knelt alertly. Immediately his slim, sensitive fingers began their skillful manipulation of the dial. For Beau Quicksilver was as expert in the unlocking of the modern safe as he was in the unraveling of cryptic crime. He brought out from a leather case a tiny stethoscope, whose diaphragm was most delicately constructed to reproduce each indicative sound from protesting safe tumblers.

The magic hand of the master sleuth soon accomplished its purpose. The door of the strong box gave forth a telltale click. Quicksilver flung the steel barrier wide. Like an eager ferret he bored into the interior. Cartman continued to stare at him as though hypnotized.

Not until Quicksilver had searched several pigeonholes was his investigation rewarded.

"Ah!" he ejaculated, holding up a packet of papers. "Excellent! We're 'most there, Cartman."

The chief strode to Quicksilver's side. His bucolic glance swept over the mass of manuscript.

"Looks like a copy for a book," he vouchsafed tentatively.

"It is," retorted Quicksilver. "It's a treatise on certain unknown facts revealing the secrets of the Nile. It will revolutionize present day fallacies concerning the lost land of the Pharaohs."

"But what," began the chief, "has it to do with Mark Amesbury's mysterious death?"

"Much," rapped out Quicksilver laconically, placing the script in his leather portfolio and swinging the safe door shut.

Then the mercurial mystery master stood stock still in the middle of the professor's chamber of historical horrors. His lightning glance played about the room. From object to object it flashed with a searing, ferreting scrutiny from which nothing could escape.

Suddenly Beau Quicksilver plunged toward a small mummy-case which enwrapped the shrunken, leather-like body of a tiny Egyptian princess. Cartman, clumsy though he was, was shortly at Quicksilver's elbow.

To the police head's amazement Quicksilver brought out a powerful lens and studied the exterior of the mummy-case with extraordinary care.

At first disappointment was plainly discernible in his features. But finally he gave an exultant shout.

A slender digit pointed at a yellow ochre hieroglyphic near the foot of the mummy-case.

"What do you see?" inquired Quicksilver with boyish enthusiasm.

Doggedly Cartman took the microscope and examined the indicated cryptic figure staring out in dull ochre from its dead brown background.

Persistently Cartman scrutinized the chrome hieroglyphic. At last he shook his massive head futilely.

"I see nothing but a heathen sign, Quicksilver, like the others."

"Examine the one by it," demanded Quicksilver. "Don't you notice anything different?"

Scrupulously Cartman complied.

"I see," he answered slowly, "that the hieroglyphic about which you are so excited appears blistered. The others do not."

"Precisely," agreed Quicksilver. *"Blistering tongues of hell,* Cartman. They licked out the life of Mark Amesbury. Now to the museum. At double quick time."

"Say, Quicksilver," remarked the chief, when they were en route to the curio zoo in the big roadster, "you've blistered my curiosity all right. But for the life of me I haven't the glimmer of an idea. Can't you drop a spark or two?"

Quicksilver smiled enigmatically.

"The whole diabolical drama will certainly be unrolled in a few moments. Now wait."

Not another word passed between the two until the big car stopped before the white marble pile of the museum.

After some parleying the satellites of the law were shown into the sumptuous private office of the assistant curator, Professor Malotti.

The noted Egyptologist was a man of Amesbury's age, tall, cadaverous, stoop-shouldered. His close-set, black eyes glinted out from the bridge of a high-arched, thin-nostrilled Roman nose. His mouth made a straight line beneath it. From his shining, hairless head to the pronounced Adam's apple in his throat the skin appeared like yellowed, wrinkled parchment— as though he had delved so long in the must and the dust of the ages that he had assimilated it into his very physiognomy.

"Well, gentlemen," his suave, carefully modulated voice greeted them, "a most unexpected pleasure. I am, however, at a loss to understand the reason for your visit to me, a stupid old fellow, who knows little of contemporary affairs or those pertaining to criminal investigation."

"Professor Malotti," cut in Quicksilver, without preamble, "Amesbury's death was clever, but *not clever enough.*"

"Sir!" responded the Italian without batting an eyelash. "That is an odd statement for a criminal investigator to make to a harmless old Egyptologist."

"Professor Malotti," retorted Quicksilver, "subterfuge is useless before blighting facts. I know how Amesbury came to his death, hastened there by the diabolical intention of a rival investigator into the secret history of old Egypt. The motive has been easy to establish. Mark Amesbury knew too much concerning ancient Egyptian lore for the peace of mind of a rival investigator. Professional jealousy and a fanatical greed to possess alone certain facts of Egyptology sent Mark Amesbury prematurely to his death."

"Indeed!" commented the professor, "May I ask why my poor, deluded, half-crazed friend crawled within an old mummy-case to die?"

"Amesbury was queer, a bit of a fanatic, I judge. To him the relics of old Egypt were sacred. He liked to bury himself in an aura of the ancient Nile. So it was his custom to take a late afternoon nap inside a certain mummy-case—as you know, Professor Malotti. His servants have so testified."

"And what if I did know it?" inquired Malotti evenly. "Really, sir, I cannot fathom the purport of your rather insinuating remarks to me, Amesbury's most intimate friend and associate."

Quicksilver shrugged. "You soon will," he answered. "Now that I have established *motive*, let me indicate the diabolical *means* by which Mark Amesbury came to his death. The thing was clever. But sometimes even tongues of hell can tattle. They did in this weird drama. And they left tiny blisters to whisper the criminal truth."

Professor Malotti's control was admirable. But the line of his jaw assumed a bluish tint.

"Blisters?" his thin lips echoed without sound. His beady, black eyes clung to Quicksilver's stern, implacable face.

"Blisters," repeated Beau Quicksilver. "For the hieroglyphics on that ancient mummy-case had been repainted, retouched by an admixture of yellow ochre and Pompeiian red—*blended with cyanide of potash.*"

Cartman gave a mighty start. Then he sat very still.

With unblinking eyes Malotti still stared insolently at Quicksilver.

The detective turned to the chief. "You get the idea? Yellow ochre and red powder mixed with cyanide disguised the potash's indicative white character and gave a fair imitation of the ancient pigments affected by the artisans of prehistoric Egypt. The admixture was daubed onto the mummy-case to freshen

up the blurred outlines of the original hieroglyphics. Amesbury
was a zealot in such symbolism. Also he was near-sighted. So
he strove to brighten up the dim characters on the death case.
He had expressed this desire to the only other great living
authority on Egyptology. And this master subtlely suggested
the ochre and Pompeiian red, both of which had been previously doctored by the insidious addition of cyanide of potash."

"B-but the blisters," protested Cartman. "And how could
cyanide of potash daubed onto the *exterior* of the mummy-case
affect the erratic crank on Egyptology?"

"Tongues of hell," repeated Quicksilver again. "For Amesbury's adviser on the retouching stunt told him to have a terrific furnace fire started—that quick drying was necessary in
order to reproduce the dull, dingy character of the ancient
hieroglyphics—to tone them down so that the modern tamper-
ing wouldn't be noticeable even to an expert."

"Yes, but—" still protested Cartman, blankly.

"The mummy-case occupied its usual dais against the big
radiator, Under the terrific heat from the radiator a deadly and
powerful quantity of cyanogen was generated and released from
the cyanide of potash. There is nothing more sure. But simul-
taneously with the letting loose of the death-dealing gas by the
high heat, the torrid atmosphere likewise caused the cyanide
of potash—salt that it is—to blister. And that whispered the
crafty truth. I have analyzed the doctored hieroglyphics on the
mummy-case. They contain cyanide of potash which has been
subjected to blistering heat."

"I still fail to see," commented Malotti sarcastically, "why you
are telling this to *me*."

"Because you are the murderer of your rival for Egyptian
honors. You plotted Amesbury's death, to which he, credulous
dolt, played into your hands with child-like gullibility. You can't
dodge the guilt, Malotti. For in your own curio room you previously tried out your diabolical death plan on a single hiero-

glyphic upon the little mummy-case enclosing an Egyptian princess."

Professor Malotti shrugged and reached swiftly toward an odd paperweight on his desk.

"None of that," cried Beau Quicksilver with a quick gesture, "I see you have neglected nothing, professor, even down to a poisoned paperweight—if the need should arise."

"Well, I'm hanged!" ejaculated Cartman, staring dazedly from Beau Quicksilver to the blanched, guilt-written face of the professor. "Can you beat it? And in the twentieth century, too! Well, I'm golblasted! Hanged if I'm not! Tongues of hell with a vengeance! Whew!"

MURDER INCOGNITO

CORNWELL SCOTT WAS dead—unnaturally dead. Yet the local authorities holding jurisdiction over the place of his demise saw nothing suspicious in his sudden, unexpected end. To them Cornwell Scott had merely departed this life prematurely, hastily and violently. They felt no further compunctions concerning his *hic jacet*. So they perfunctorily wrote finis on the affair of his taking-off and turned their square-toed minds to jazzier criminal jousts. Cornwell Scott was merely unnaturally dead—quite so.

However, old Dame Nemesis thought otherwise. *She* was not asleep at the retribution switch.

Hence:

A scarlet and black speedster halted at the curb of a somnolent, suburban street. Two men emerged—haste written in their every movement.

The taller put out a finger-tip preparatory to pushing the button on a brown stone fronted house. Yet before any ring could be registered, the door yawned. A gray-clad servant stood there like some bristling, old bird spreading invisible, protecting wings against any hasty intrusion.

"We must see Quicksilver at once," began the taller of the pair arrogantly, attempting to push by. "Matter of the utmost moment."

"Mr. Quicksilver can't be disturbed needlessly," answered Shunta, like a well-wound up marionette. "He just told the chief of police to go to the—t-t-that he couldn't be bothered," finished Shunta lamely.

"Huh!" snapped the pompous newcomer. "I'm no four-figure minion of the law! Weighty private matter at Quicksilver's own figure. I'm Parris Letherway," he added with the manner of one who confers a mighty favor by the mere mouthing of the awe-inspiring cognomen.

Letherway was a financier *de luxe* in the world of affairs. Even Shunta, the wary, buffeting serving-man of the enigmatic Beau Quicksilver knew the commercial rating of the man before him.

Shunta bowed diffidently.

"The servant of a Roman prince was sent away this morning," he murmured apologetically. "Mr. Quicksilver is particular about those whom he serves. He didn't like the fellow's livery. Said the master who could stand a get-up like that around him wouldn't know a real crime if it was pinned on him. I am afraid, sir—"

A buzzer sounded from the speaking-tube above the bell. "Shunta," Quicksilver's languid voice floated down, "ask Mr. Letherway to pencil his business on his card. If the bare outline interests me, I'll hear the full facts. Otherwise," coolly, "I prefer to meditate on the obtuse outcroppings of crime—and the frailty of the canniest criminal."

"Well, I like his nerve," growled Letherway, red to the ears. "I'm damned if a silk-and-linen manikin I could blow off his feet with one breath is going to treat me like a lackey!" He wheeled away apoplectically.

Letherway's companion hastily touched his irascible associate's elbow. He sank his voice to a whisper.

"It's too incredible for any one to touch but Quicksilver. To be sure, he's everything that's sphinxlike and tantrumish. Regular riddle himself. But why split hairs over his personal idiosyncrasies? He has a Bradstreet reputation for delivering the goods in record-breaking time. You're a fool, Letherway, to fly into a fury just because the fellow is finical and difficult to interest. He toes no traditional track. He's a pioneer in a hackneyed field."

Swallowing his hasty choler, Letherway, with none too good a grace, yanked out a fountain-pen and a card. He wrote with his mouth shut to a grim, straight line.

CHAPTER II

WHILE THIS DOORSTEP vaudeville was being pulled on the mat before Quicksilver's domicile, the detective squatted on all-fours, examining with profound attention a magnificent Kurdish rug which covered the floor of his den. The rug was an imported affair, woven in the rich, warm symbolism peculiar to the bold and warring dwellers on the Euphrates, the Highlanders of Turkey. Caressingly Quicksilver sank his slender fingers into the thick pile of the rug. One sensed the delicacy of the digits. Yet that same number eight hand packed a wallop which had sent more than one roughneck reeling back in groggy surprise. For Quicksilver was a master of many arts—not the least of which was the art of self-defense. What his one hundred and fifty-five pounds lacked in mere bulk he made up in muscular adeptness and cometlike speed.

Penn Markham, Quicksilver's side-kick in criminal cases, squatted on a chair by the table, busy with a chess-board. But Markham's interest flagged. He wondered what new mystery might even now be perching on their very threshold.

But Quicksilver was deaf to any prospective enigma. He didn't carry a one-track mind under the glossy mane of dark hair which topped his keen features. But he could concentrate on one thing whenever he wished to do so.

"Penn, old top," drawled Quicksilver from his quadruped position on the floor, followed by an aggravating pause.

Markham strained forward intently. He hoped that the at times irritating aloofness of his companion would be broken by some casual comment on the money magnate who was now almost humbly striving to pen his entrance into Quicksilver's interest and good graces. Again Markham was doomed to disappointment. Quicksilver's moods never could be pigeonholed. They spattered off in a hundred unexpected directions.

Seemingly entirely oblivious of Letherway and his possible claim to parking a real crime, Quicksilver remarked, "Odd things, ancient rugs. Like people. Have the record of many obtuse tales woven into their warp and woof, even as individu-

als are but the warp and woof of thought and environment. Penn, old boy, d'you ever think that every mystery is made up of symbols—that into the warp and woof of each crime is woven—not the history of a race, as in the rug, but the character of an individual?"

Penn Markham shifted impatiently. He pushed the pawns on the board abruptly away. "Aw, Quixie, you make me tired! Where is your curiosity with a new case stalking on your very door-mat?"

Quicksilver shrugged his perfectly tailored shoulders. But he continued his aggravating examination of the rug.

"Bah!" he retorted. "Most mysteries are stale before they are committed! Even spraying them with Letherway's gold-dust combined with skunk-oil would fail to give them intriguing atmosphere."

A knock fluttered on the door. Seemingly deaf to it, Quicksilver poised his lens over a red, geometric figure on the priceless Kurd. With profound leisure the mystery-master at last straightened up. As though it were a physical effort, he sank into a huge, upholstered chair.

"Come in, Shunta," he invited lackadaisically.

The shadowy figure of Shunta opened the door with expert noiselessness. Then he shut it as quietly. He had long ago learned that noise was taboo in that brown stone apartment where mysterious people came and went.

"Now let's see that card," drawled Quicksilver, as he lighted a monogrammed cigarette from his omnipresent silver smoke-case.

Shunta tendered it and then backed with weasel-like swiftness against the door through which he had come. Only a tiny clock on the mantel shelf ticked unconcernedly on. It alone seemed magnificently unafraid of Quicksilver's masquerading moods.

Letherway had written:

> Cornwell Scott is dead at the lodge on Scott's Island. The local boobs set his demise down as suicide. *But I know better!* I am prepared to swear that a foul and subtle murder has been screened behind the cloak of self-destruction. Give me a few moments of your time to convince you that it is a case for an expert in criminology.
>
> LETHERWAY.

Introspectively Quicksilver drummed on the bristol-board. Yet no muscle of his face had changed. But some of the lassitude of his former languor had seeped away. There was a hidden suggestion of budding hope about him. Penn Markham was quick to sense the slow-dawning of reawakened interest. What Markham did not deduce was that Quicksilver had been a bit pleased by the tribute paid him by the moneymaker downstairs.

He knew that Letherway wasn't the type to mouth saccharine encomiums idly.

"Show the gentlemen up, Shunta."

There was no wait between the acts of the fast shaping drama. Again Shunta knocked with ghostly gentleness. At Quicksilver's mandate he threw the door wide.

"Mr. Letherway and Mr. Ellery," he announced in a monotonous, low voice.

Then he withdrew like the neutral shadow that he was.

Under his bristling brows Letherway studied the foppish figure before him. He was a reader of men. For once a bantam-weight specimen of the *genus homo* did not arouse the usual scorn displayed by the big man for the featherweight. In an enlightening flash Letherway set Quicksilver down as a super-poseur concealing a Napoleonic nerve under his debonair purple and fine linen. There was an aura of dynamic energy radiating from the exquisite, lolling figure. Letherway was a master poker-player. He knew the value of convincing bluff.

"You've heard of Markham," observed Quicksilver casually. "Roll up the chairs there. Smoke?"

As he passed over his cigarette-case, Perm Markham stared at him in unfeigned amazement. Something had once more magically transformed his friend into an affable human being. He was no longer a chilling thinking-machine.

"Give me the affair from the outset," he requested as he expelled slow wreaths of smoke.

Letherway leaned forward—an unlighted cigarette between his fingers. Quicksilver's eyes narrowed to pin points of tempered steel. He no longer lolled. Something in Letherway's strung-up air had communicated itself to the sleuth.

"Scott invited five of us to his lodge on his island—twenty miles out. You know the place. Wild, solitary rocks, heavy growth of pine. The lodge is the only habitation on the island, a magnificent structure of half-logs, rustic without forgetting modern comforts."

Quicksilver nodded. "Scott's Castle," as the place was called, was a show-spot, the whim of a high-powered financier.

"We were among those present," went on Letherway. "Give you the others later. Scott was keen on poker, so cooked up a stag party at the lodge. We passed two days there uneventfully—the invitation was for a week. On the third morning an excited alarm was given. A servant stumbled on the truth. Scott's den was found locked. Practically hermetically sealed. Get that? The transom was tightly closed when I climbed up to it. Works only from the inside, you understand—not for air, but for light." The room was unlighted by artificial illumination. But the morning sun was sufficient to reveal the figure of Scott apparently sagged back asleep in a heavy upholstered chair near a gas jet. He had one peculiarity. He insisted on gas—without any kind of a shade or a hint of a Welsbach. Said the flaring jets intensified the rustic atmosphere of the lodge. Seemed like medieval torches.

We broke in quickly. But before we got the door opened we smelled escaping gas. And a hint of the truth had percolated into our staggered minds. There's little more to tell. Scott lay dead in his chair. He appeared as though he slept peacefully. The room reeked with gas, which the wide-open jet must have been belching ever since it was turned to Scott's undoing. There wasn't a thing in the room that whispered of anything but suicide. No one could possibly have entered, nor could accident be considered. Scott was super-careful. He had all the windows closed and securely bolted—the nights there are cold. The single door was treble locked—absolutely untampered with, with the key and bolt on the inside and a chain in position, too. Scott often slept on the couch in his den all night. And he was a bit of a coward. Rather a nut on keeping behind plenty of bolts and locks at night.

"We notified the local authorities in whose domain the island falls. They gave the room a careful search. There was not a thing but shouted of suicide. Scott had been dead some hours when found. The local authorities have made out a death certificate for suicide from asphyxiation. How could they do otherwise with a man found almost hermetically sealed in his own den with the gas jet turned on full?"

"All this is everyday tragedy," cut in Quicksilver, a bit peevishly. "Just why do you think Scott did not commit suicide?"

The big man leaned forward as though fearing some unseen ear. He sank his voice to an impressive whisper.

"Mr. Quicksilver, I knew Scott well. We have launched many a double-headed deal together. Few men valued his life as he."

Quicksilver nodded. "The bolts bear out this statement of yours. Proceed."

Some of Quicksilver's impatient air had been dissipated before these words. He leaned forward, his poise alert, nay, almost exultant. The glint of a smile flickered over his former bored features.

"Another thing," went on Letherway. "Scott loathed suicide—considered it a cardinal crime. He was a fanatic on this point."

"The urge of some mighty internal force forecasting a catastrophe might have changed his opinion," suggested Quicksilver.

Curtly Letherway shook his head in negation. "No," he retorted. "I was in Scott's confidence. I happen to know that he was on the point of putting through a tremendously important deal within a week. Never in his life was his physical well-being more imperative than for this weighty affair, which has now, by his sudden demise, been irrevocably forestalled."

Beau Quicksilver sat up rigidly. His eyes were glued to Letherway's earnest face. Darts of light smoldered in the detective's deep-set orbs.

"Ah," he rapped out, "the thing grows interesting. A motive for murder now appears—murder under the cloak of suicide. Just who were being entertained under Scott's roof, in addition to you and Mr. Ellery here?"

"The other three were Dallas, the banker, Marshall, the broker, and Harvey, the copper magnate—all imposing figures in financial circles, as you will readily recognize."

Beau Quicksilver glanced quickly at the clock, an imported affair on the big fireplace mantel.

With the return to his occasional flares of irascibility he demanded, "Why didn't you phone before now? Much valuable time has been lost."

"Tried to. Could arouse no one."

Quicksilver shrugged. "The line into the chief of police's sanctum is by no means silent," he suggested tartly. "I suppose the body has been removed from the den and that the death room remains both unlocked and unguarded. Undoubtedly the guests have gone their several ways, since suicide gives no legal excuse for holding them."

"That's the hell of it," acknowledged Letherway ruefully. "Naturally with such an open-and-shut appearance of suicide they couldn't be held. And if murder has been done, as I positively believe, it is well to arouse no suspicions."

"Good idea," commented Quicksilver. "Undoubtedly there would be little to discover on the body since the means of death has been carefully ascertained. They couldn't bungle that with the vomiting gas jet in the room. I wish the den could have been kept under surveillance."

Letherway smiled craftily. "Scott has in his employ one of my ex-servants. Fellow with me fifteen years—regular Gibraltar of dependability. I tipped him off to keep an eye on the room until my return."

"Good enough!" shot out Quicksilver, "Just a moment and I'll be with you. Markham, while I fall into my motor togs, rustle out the Greyhound. Letherway, we'll be trailing the heels of your rouge-et-noir speed-gig in the flip of an eye."

Like a whirlwind of energy, Quicksilver's lithe-strung figure torpedoed itself from the room. Markham had already gone out to the garage for the sleuth's big gray roadster.

"Queer combination of twaddle and pose, that fellow," remarked Ellery.

Letherway shrugged. "Twaddle or craft, I'm not yet prepared

to take my so-help-me on which. Are you? The fellow baffles me. Think I have him pigeonholed, and then he slips out of my fingers just like—quicksilver."

The detective now reappeared, clad in khaki. He wore heavy tortoise-rimmed spectacles. They changed his facial expression unbelievably. For he was dressed in the habiliments of a snappy chauffeur.

"Now, Mr. Letherway," he said, "let me drive you in your car. Markham will push along Ellery in the Greyhound. Then he'll bring my car back from the pier. As your chauffeur, I'll arouse no comment from the servants or from any suspicious pair of eyes which may still be watching warily at the island. Suppose you give me an outline of everything that happened from your arrival at the lodge. Nothing too trivial to recall. Something may develop from the most casual remembrance. Let's go!"

CHAPTER III

THE CLOT OF green in the leaping waters now resolved itself into a charming wooded island. A close-up disclosed the spot to be a considerable property with melancholy evergreens waving somber plumes against the sky.

The dead millionaire's power-boat nosed expertly to the landing. Two Great Danes came tearing down to the tiny pier. Their vehement woof-woofs echoed and re-echoed about the eerie island.

Letherway commented as the three stepped quickly ashore, in a tone for Quicksilver's ear alone. "Another proof of Scott's super-caution for his health. The dogs have the run of the place at night. It would be practically impossible for any prowler to make a surreptitious landing without the Danes megaphoning an alarm. Down, Raffles! Down, Wolf!" he admonished the dogs.

But the Great Danes kept up an uproarious duet at the heels of the trio.

The lodge itself now appeared, constructed of half-logs which had been weathered a pleasing brown. The roof glimmered forth, a deep scarlet, surrounded by the plumed tree-tops. Whimsically, Quicksilver thought that its sides might have been dyed in blood, since scarlet was the symbol of subtle violence.

They entered a side door, closely canopied by shadowing trees. They walked through a short corridor ending in a considerable square hall, topped by a huge glass dome. For the thick-growing trees and the pristine wildness of the creepers and foliage surrounding the place made the overhead skylight imperative. Heavily paneled doors lighted by transoms cut this interior center court. One door in a corner displayed a heavy smashed panel, temporarily repaired.

A man busy with a duster looked up at their entrance. A brief, understanding glance and a negative shake of his head told them that nothing suspicious had occurred in the death-room.

By previous agreement Letherway at this point spoke for the benefit of the servant.

"Now, Jacques," he addressed the pseudo-chauffeur, "before my bags are packed, just step in here a minute with me. There are some road-maps in the table drawer I want you to go over."

"*Oui, monsieur,*" answered Quicksilver, as he followed Letherway into the death-chamber.

The moment they were inside Quicksilver seemed to forget absolutely the presence of his companion. Letherway remained at the door, his eyes on the famous crime-chaser.

Beau Quicksilver stood rigidly in the center of the room. He appeared as immobile as a mandarin, except for his darting glances and his quivering nostrils. Be seemed to be sniffing the atmosphere of the place. The chamber still smelled faintly of gas. It was square in shape and sizable. Half-logs ran from the floor to the rather low ceiling. There were brilliant colorful rugs on the walls which gave a bizarre, rich effect. The dominant colors of red and black were repeated in the soft, thick pile covering the polished floor. Quicksilver knew rugs. His eyes went directly to a magnificent Kurdish specimen over the mantel-shelf with its small mahogany clock. This rug was by far the finest of the lot and must have cost a breath-taking figure. Even the heavy shadows dimming the region of the fireplace could not hide this fact.

Quicksilver's coursing glance encircled the room. The furniture was sparse. There were several upholstered chairs and a big mahogany table near one wall, cluttered with magazines and books. Close to this table stood the big chair in which Scott had slept his last.

Quicksilver examined the lighting system. In addition to the long arm above the table which had snuffed out Scott's life there were four other wall-jets and a big chandelier in the center of the room. He scrutinized the death-jet. Yet it told him nothing. He studied the locks on the two big windows opposite the fireplace end of the room and found them entirely competent. And reputable witnesses had sworn that both were carefully fastened when the body was discovered. The vines and the foliage outside were undisturbed, eliminating the windows from consideration.

The detective next subjected the door to a grilling study. Letherway spoke the truth. The dead man had taken no chances with his personal safety. For the door carried an impregnable lock, a tempered steel bolt, and a chain. All of these had been fastened when entrance had been forced, making human ingress absolutely impossible. No wonder the local authorities had returned the verdict of suicide.

Quicksilver next gave the room a foot-by-foot once-over for any skipped clue. From object to object he darted with unswerving energy. He even tapped all the walls for sign of some unsuspected trap-door affording secret access. Yet there was nothing even remotely suspicious.

With a dexterous twist of one supple wrist, he swung a heavy, upholstered chair to a spot beneath the transom. Letherway began to sense the trained muscles masquerading under the debonair exterior. Quicksilver flung the chair into place without the slightest trace of effort. From the chair he examined the transom, a duplicate of the others opening on the square hall. It operated by the usual hinged rod, parallel to the door-casing. The only difference was that the hinges had been so set that the swiveling curtain of glass could be tipped to yawn not more than an inch on the inside. It was a physical impossibility for anything to enter the room by the transom, even had it been open when the dead body was discovered. But the transom was found tightly closed, else the escaping gas would have broadcasted a warning of the impending tragedy within.

In a brown study Beau Quicksilver replaced the chair. Slowly his eyes retraveled the confines of the room as though by dint of sheer will power he would drag forth some whispering atom of the truth. The den was singularly dark. The pall of death seemed to shroud it. His glance volleyed to the clock on the fireplace mantel, suddenly curious as to the passing of time, and he stepped closer to it.

Then Beau Quicksilver stood rigidly motionless. His eyes clung persistently to the white face of the timepiece.

For the hands of the death-clock stood at 1:10.

Quicksilver consulted his own watch. It registered five minutes past ten.

Slowly his darting eyes narrowed to gleaming slits of light. For the first time he seemed to be aware of Letherway's presence.

"Was the clock in this room running when Scott entered it last night?"

Letherway's big head jerked up. "It was. I was talking with Scott here at five minutes to ten last evening. I remember distinctly glancing at the timepiece just previous to my departure."

"So," observed Quicksilver slowly, "the clock was running as usual when you left the room at ten. Did any one else see him after that?"

"No one. The local authorities went through that rigmarole."

Something in Quicksilver's steady glance finally percolated Letherway's attention. Hypnotically his eyes went to the clock on the mantel. Dead silence ensued—a potent, bristling silence.

"Why, it stopped at 1:10!" ejaculated Letherway. "At 1:10!"

"And it's fully wound up," stated Beau Quicksilver meaningly.

"Then it could not have run down," Letherway rejoined. "By Jove, Quicksilver, do you suppose that 1:10 means anything? No one can tell for a certainty at what moment life passed out of Scott's body. That depends on the lung space and the flow of gas. What in thunder does the clock stalled at 1:10 mean then?"

"It means that we may be at the first thread of the tangle," responded Quicksilver.

He leaned heavily against the mantelshelf, his elbow resting on it, lost in profound thought. The frown between his brows intensified. Suddenly he brought his fist down on the mantel.

"Letherway," he began, "how—"

But he never finished the sentence. He stood riveted like a man who sees a ghost, a specter of retarded retribution.

Thick, secretive silence no longer brooded over the room. An insidious new sound broke its former stillness. Through the chamber of death resounded the reawakened tick-tick-tick from the previously silent clock on the shelf.

"Huh, the clock's started up again!" observed Letherway casually. "Temperamental things, clocks. Skittish as a horse."

Quicksilver did not answer. His former balked attitude had dropped from him. He leaned forward like a runner awaiting the crack of the pistol. A spark gleamed from his eyes. Full well did he know that the blow he had casually struck on the shelf might be the first for dissipating the mystery. To the ordinary investigator the mere fortuity of what his movement had set in motion might mean nothing. Quicksilver was not the casual sleuth. He read into the handwriting on the wall a startling possibility. It was for him to make a waterproof analogy and apply it.

He stared at the magnificent Kurdish rug above the mantelpiece. With peculiar intentness he noted that the bit of weaving was by far the finest in the room—that there was no other covering comparable with it, either in coloring or in the thickness of the pile.

"Letherway," rapped out Quicksilver, "just phone Markham to be at the pier in an hour. I am about finished here."

As the money-magnate's back was shut from the room Quicksilver lunged like an arrow to the Kurdish rug over the mantelpiece.

CHAPTER IV

ON THE FIRST mail the following morning a small, square box was delivered at the private office of the addressee. The man at the plain oak desk had one business peculiarity. He insisted that he open all personal mail himself without recourse to the services of a secretary.

With methodical precision he went through his mail, ultimately arriving at the tiny box. He broke its seal, his eyes still on a business communication atop the desk. A plain white box emerged. Within was a bed of cotton. Poking in two investigating digits, the man at the desk separated the downy wad. But he made no further movement. With rigid intentness his eyes remained glued to a small object within.

The buzzer sounded at his elbow. But he appeared deaf to sound. He sat like a graven image, staring pop-eyed at what confronted him from within the tiny box. Not until an attendant had knocked twice on the door marked "Private" did the man at the desk rouse himself from his narcotized state. As he bade the knocker enter he hastily deposited the box and its contents far in the bottom of a trouser pocket. Then he bit his lips as the door yawned for the day's business.

The next morning an ordinary looking manila envelope was

ripped open by the man behind the desk. He had heaved a
mighty sigh of relief when his nervous furtive scrutiny of the
morning's mail revealed no tiny registered box. But he gave a
mighty start when a small object—a twin of the one which had
first come in the box—now rolled accusingly forth from an
ordinary envelope.

Again the man behind the desk sat motionless. But the
muscles around his mouth twitched. And a sickly pallor had
sponged the habitual color from his features. Into his eyes crept
the look of a haunted, caged animal, fighting some insidious,
hidden force. With a snarl, half bestial, half desperate, he took
the object between his shaking fingers and hid it away in his
clothing.

"Boss looking a little ragged to-day," remarked a man in the
outer office. "Jumpy and fidgety. Thought he was a regular icicle.
Wonder what's causing the thaw? Guess he's in for a spell of
sickness."

The man behind the plain oak desk was in for a spell of
sickness—a nauseating, gnawing, growing terror.

So day after day, for a week, the man behind the oak desk
received without fail a duplicate of that hateful object which
had come to him so stealthily, so significantly, encased in the
tiny box on that first fateful morning. There was no telling how
the thing might come. Once he had found it on his bread-plate
in a restaurant; again it appeared on the edge of his desk-
blotter upon his arrival at the office. And his roaring fury roused
nothing but scornful denials from those whom he questioned.
No one could tell him how the thing had come.

Finally a man stopped him on a busy downtown street, an
ultra-respectable dignified old gentleman with perfectly cropped
Van Dyke and immaculate Prince Albert.

"Excuse me, sir," the old boy interrupted him courteously,
"but didn't you just drop this?"

Into the startled palm of the man facing him the whiskered
stranger dropped another of those accursed objects which were

destroying his sleep, nipping his appetite and sapping his nerves. When he faced about like an enraged bull, the courteous stranger had gone, sucked into thin air. A mighty shiver shook the man on the pavement. He recalled the knowing look in the bearded stranger's eyes and the sarcastic, insinuating note in the overtly polite question.

Shivering like one with the ague he was driven home in a taxi, hoping desperately that his own four walls would grant him sanctuary from the accursed hounding things which had daily found him out by some unforeseen hook or crook. He knew that dark forces were moving, swiftly but certainly, to his undoing. He knew that somewhere, somehow, some one had hit upon the nerve-racking truth.

He telephoned from his home that he was ill, that he wouldn't be down to the office again that day. He remained closeted in his room, jabbing the bell at intervals for heavy libations of Scotch to brace his jumping nerves.

Some time later a servant tapped diffidently on his door. "Mr. Letherway's here, sir, with a friend. Got a big opening. Wants your O.K. on it. Got a fine opportunity for big returns."

The man in the huge chair by the window looked at his servant with bloodshot eyes. His face was flushed. But his lips were pale.

"Tell them to come up and make it brief," he growled. "I am a sick man, but I can't pass up big business."

"Yes, sir," bowed the servant, and he returned with Letherway and a dapper, snappily clad, young Frenchman, who twirled his mustache and adjusted his monocle.

"This is Count de Grace from Baron von Gothshild," Letherway announced.

"Be seated, gentlemen," greeted the man with the flushed face, thickly. "Just what is the business deal you have in the wind?"

The dapper count leaned forward, as though to impart a weighty secret. His hand shot out beneath the very nose of the man in the chair. And on its palm rested a diabolical, small object.

"You haven't a leg to stand on, Linyard Marshall," rapped out Quicksilver, his faked accent banished. "I know how you killed Scott. I know that you screened the means of a crafty crime behind the gift of a valuable Kurdish rug in order to make Scott's demise appear like ordinary self-destruction. You see, I have discovered the reason for the gift rug."

Marshall, the big broker and supposed friend of the dead man, slowly arose from his chair with an odd, jerky movement. His wide, glassy stare never left the object on Quicksilver's outstretched palm. His lips worked horribly. Inch by inch he fell away from the accusing article. Then he collapsed suddenly into his chair. The barrage of grim objects which had daily confronted him had rifled his control and smashed his nerve. The accusing thing on the outstretched palm before him was but the final straw.

"T-t-take your d-d-damned hand away," he blubbered. "Stop sticking your p-p-proof in my face! You've got me all right. Take that damned thing away! I d-d-did it. I confess. What more do you want?"

With that he fell in a helpless heap.

CHAPTER V

"SIMPLE, YOU SEE," explained Beau Quicksilver to Letherway some time later. "After the house had retired Marshall merely stood on a chair in the darkened hall and waited until Scott slept in his chair in the den. Contrary to the way it was found, Marshall had seen to it that the transom was left open an inch for his purpose. So he merely poised through the inch opening the barrel of a twenty-two caliber revolver equipped with a silencer. The long-armed gas jet inside was turned so that it stood in direct alignment with the thick Kurdish rug over the fireplace. The murderer drew a bead on the lighted jet above the sleeping Scott and fired, instantly snuffing out the gas. The bullet sped into the black, thick pile of the Kurdish rug, embedding itself in the log behind. The thick stuff of the rug instantly closed over the small circle, making the bullet-hole absolutely invisible. I found the bullet in the log behind the rug.

"I ascertained that the transom may be worked shut from the outside by pushing smartly against the sash, although it cannot be opened in this manner. So the killer next pushed the transom shut, leaving the sleeping Scott to his fate under the snuffed jet with its belching fumes. But in the darkness the clock—literally shocked—stopped ticking. When the bullet hurtled itself into the rug and the wood behind the shelf, it must have set in motion some slight vibration which stopped the delicately attuned timepiece. The possibility hit me over the head when I chanced to start the clock as I whacked the shelf smartly with my fist. Instantly I knew that some form of concussion might have stalled the timepiece at 1:10—the precise instant when a dastardly crime was set in motion under the screen of suicide.

"You know how I hounded Marshall for a week with the presentation of a twenty-two caliber bullet. Your recollection that Marshall, known to be a cardinal miser, brought Scott the priceless Kurdish rug as a gift, set me to thinking. When I dug it out of you that it was Marshall's suggestion for the dead man to replace the ordinary Smyrna over the mantel with the Kurd, I again smelled a rat. All the Smyrnas in the room carry a short, wiry pile or nap, which would not spring back to normal appearance if anything touched their surfaces. The evidence of the rug against Marshall was purely circumstantial, although I also learned from you that Scott's purported deal was inimical to Marshall's interest. Hence I pulled the hounding-bullet ordeal."

"Lucky you whacked that shelf," murmured Letherway.

"Luck is merely a matter of interpretation and application," answered Beau Quicksilver, thoughtfully. "The started clock told *you* nothing. My blow on the shelf merely speeded up the solution and the denouement. For I would have dug up the answer to that silenced clock if I'd had to camp in the room for a month!"

"I believe you," answered Letherway heartily.